David Stuart is a retired teacher who has lived and taught in Nigeria, Wales and Lincolnshire. He is a widower with two daughters and two grandchildren, twins. For the last 25 years, he has taught Creative Writing for WEA and recently on line for the deaf. His interests are Classical Music, Poetry and Travel especially more recently the armchair variety.

To my wife, Jacque, and daughters, Catherine and Marion.

David Stuart

CONVERSATIONS WITH THE LANDSCAPE

AUSTIN MACAULEY PUBLISHERS

LONDON • CAMBRIDGE • NEW YORK • SHARJAH

A CIP catalogue record for this title is available from the British Library.

ISBN 9781035879212 (Paperback)
ISBN 9781035879229 (ePub e-book)

www.austinmacauley.com

First Published 2024
Austin Macauley Publishers Ltd®
1 Canada Square
Canary Wharf
London
E14 5AA

I am grateful to Michelle Calvert of the Deaf Empowerment Network (once Rare Rockets!) in Newton Aycliffe for patiently reading the relevant late chapters, and providing me with great encouragement and valuable friendship.

1
The Desert

It all started as a kind of holiday. After years behind a desk, I am out in the field again, doing some real geology. On either side of the entrance to the unnamed wadi are two crumbling sandstone and granite escarpments.

Beyond them the almost featureless desert of the Tenere, with just occasional isolate outliers. This is the Republic of Niger, quite distinct from Nigeria to the south. A vast and sparsely populated territory, once a French colony. If we are lucky, we may see nomadic groups making their way across the featureless landscape.

We three foreigners are geologists. Expedition leader and scientist/academic: Declan, with his two assistants: myself and John. To complete the party: two soldiers, Yusuf and Gabriel, and then Ahmed, our cook. And you might ask what we are up to. Quite innocent research: desert erosion and sedimentation especially in the dry steep-sided valleys called "wadis" on the Tenere margins. For John and I, this is almost a holiday. Before retirement, we had been stuck for many years behind desks in Britain working for an oil company.

Geology on paper. Now, at long last, we are back here in the field, doing some of the real stuff and more specifically, geomorphology. A big boys' adventure. Just a few steps up from building sand castles on the beach, some people would say. But at least we are demonstrating that for some of us, research can be fun.

We drove here in two big Toyotas. We are equipped with two splendidly comfortable tents and lots of gadgets: augurs, electronic equipment, radios and computers. A gas-fired frig and cooker, with a small generator for charging up equipment and laptops. The two Nigerian soldiers are here to guard us; it's not clear what from, but they were allocated by the Nigerian government in some arrangement with the Niger authorities.

Ahmed is here to feed us. He's a devout Muslim, a local who speaks Arabic, and so will be able to converse with the Tuareg nomads if we by chance encounter them. We are not very likely to, and they will probably avoid us. I speak some French, enough to get us by, should the situation arise.

The whole expedition has been organised by our leader, Declan, from his university in California. The three of us were fellow students in Britain thirty years ago. I suppose we all have been bitten in some way by the allure of the desert. However, the outcome of our expedition is going to exceed the reach of our wildest imaginations.

Declan has been engaged for some years in research into how wadis and escarpments are weathered and eroded, and the nature of deposited material (pediment) which accumulates. He has done work on this in Arizona and the Kalahari. Even though he was born in England, he now has the gentlest of Californian accents, no more than a purr which seems to match his height at well over six feet. The work being undertaken here is part of an ongoing project involving the use of sensory electronic equipment to investigate and chart what lies under the floor of the wadi, at the foot of scarp and cliffs, and on the desert floor in the drainage basins that lie beyond the wadis. Potentially quite dull work unless you are an enthusiast.

Declan handles most of the technical electronic side single-handedly. John and I are allocated the more mundane task of sampling a network of drill holes using small augurs, taking measurements and samples from various depths. 'It's always good to have some first-hand data, as a back-up,' says Declan weighing a chunk of the dusty rock in his hand as if it were some tactile indicator.

'Puts some real hands-on geology into the whole project,' with a grin. 'You're the boss!' says Philip even though the relationship between us has never assumed that kind of hierarchy.

We sometimes even get the chance to work turn and turn about with the electronic equipment and the sampling. The two soldiers sit around and stare at the landscape while they smoke. Boredom drives them to ask if they can help in any way with the augurs which is pretty routine stuff. The cook Ahmed rarely interferes, standing aloof from it. Almost as if it were something distasteful or unclean.

We flew into Kano, Nigeria, a few days ago and then were brought by military plane to Zinder in Niger. There we picked up the two vehicles and some equipment along with the soldiers and Ahmed, before driving north 450 kilometres to Agades in the heart of the desert. Two days on a road which switched between a thin strip of tar, corrugated crushed laterite, and blown sand. At one point, a dry river bed, about as wide as the Thames, was spanned by what might have been a splendid bridge.

'What happens here chief?' I asked Declan. One of the bridge arches was missing, demolished apparently during a head-on truck collision. Another lorry sat mid-river bogged down in soft sand.

A policeman came hurrying forward waving frantically and shouting, 'Via interdit. They repair the bridge tomorrow one week please.'

'Which of those?'

The man shrugged. He gestured northwards. A safer crossing higher up stream was being investigated. Our Nigerian driver, Gabriel, tried to convince us that he could make it across the sand, but we dissuaded him, even if it meant a delay. Happily, an hour or so later, someone came buzzing down the river bank with the news that a crossing higher up was indeed possible. We found ourselves eventually safely tucked into the middle of a convoy which crossed the dry river at a sort of ford.

A couple of hours later, it was the stony desert, the stuff we call "reg", stretching to a vague horizon shrouded in a heat haze. Clumps of spiny bushes dotted the landscape at intervals of a hundred yards or so. Occasionally, a troop of camels led by figures in black clothing would cross the road diagonally, their paths bearing no relation to the road we were following.

I was driving the lead Toyota. No road traffic of any kind, so I drove down the centre of the narrow strip of tar avoiding the road edges which were broken or cratered. It occurred to me that it wasn't clear to me which side of the road I had to revert to should there be any other traffic. After an hour, we saw a plume of sand ahead, indicating a truck some miles off was coming towards us. Like us, he seemed to be hugging the centre of the road. The black bulk of the truck grew larger.

'Don't like the look of this,' said John sitting by my side.

'I'll just get off the road altogether and let him through,' I said, hoping the slightly panicky feeling was not audible, and waved my intentions to Gabriel driving the vehicle behind us. The truck appeared to be maintaining the middle of the road path, but then with a lurch and a blast on the horn… as if the driver had just been woken up… it edged to its right. Wheels churned up the dust and laterite, and the plume of sand became a sandstorm which blasted our Toyotas as we tunnelled by each other. When it was over there was a final blast on the horn from the truck driver. Was that a warning? Or a farewell? Or just contempt?

'Glad he got it right,' I said.

We camped out close to the road under a black and shrouded sky with no stars visible and resumed the bone-shaking and tedious journey the next day to Agades.

Here, we enjoyed the welcome shade of the palms but had to wait for two hours while our documents and vehicles were examined. But then it came to a really gruelling part of the journey on an ill-defined track into the Air Massif with hardly any human traces of any kind. The heat was made more unpleasant by the fine-blown sand. These highlands received a little more rain than the surrounding desert, so there were stunted trees and even small patches of cultivation in depressions.

Eventually, the mountains in front became more chaotic with great granite bosses and slabs. The tallest Mount Tangak at 1800 metres. The predominant colours here were sandstone red and ochre but shot through with layers of limestone, metamorphosed by heat and pressure to silvery marble, the whole like some immense layered cake. Far to the north and west, there were workings for uranium and other minerals.

Another 500 kilometres eastward would have brought us to Tibesti Plateau in Chad with its extinct volcanic rocks, empty craters and mountains reaching up to peaks at over 3,000 metres. I had read about the region and its dramatic cave paintings of creatures like crocodiles, elephants and water birds. Evidence of wetter conditions centuries ago. The Air Massif here was similar but on a smaller scale.

We eventually drew into our wadi on the eastern flank of the Massif. Here there was virtually no vegetation, and the sandstone and granite cliffs were split and shattered into terraces and columns towering a thousand feet on each side of the wadi. Broken sand and rocks formed a pediment at forty-five degrees beneath. The dry wadi itself debouched onto the "reg" creating a level floor of what might have been the shallow saline lake. But that would be only when heavy rain clouds, on rare occasions, hit the mountains and the dry wadi became a torrent.

Beyond was the Tenere, sterile, seemingly endless with occasional lumps of rock-like sugar lumps on the horizon. Somewhere behind us Mount Tamgat but hidden by the haze. Records were sparse, but it was rumoured that rain only came every twenty to thirty years when humid clouds were cooled by ascent of the Massif. We switched off the engines and the strange silence enveloped us… even if we had spoken, our words would surely not have been audible, even if we had shouted them out. But whether announced or not, we had arrived.

2

The Rockfall

We are up early the next morning, keen to get our investigations underway. We are a hundred yards away from the wadi on the north side. Our legs and backs still ache from the jolting and juddering of the journey. Mine are still twitching as we begin to plot the positions of the augurs. The silence of our first night in the heart of the desert had been awesome, in the true sense of the word.

A black starlit sky. The only break in the silence was someone's cough. It didn't allow you to sleep. So the routine of the work we have to do is really welcome. Our plan is to work here for two weeks, moving slowly from the wadi mouth into the desert. Two sessions each day, 6:00 am to 11:00 am, then 5:00 pm until it was too dark, otherwise resting up through the middle of the day.

I have been put in charge of the daily camp routines and "logistics", and the others are happy with this; we all know each other, and it always works well that way. I wouldn't say we know that much about each other's lives in a broader sense. True, John and I worked for the same oil company. He doesn't have much to say for himself, and I'm not a great talker myself. We know only a little about each other's home lives.

My wife Alice and I have met John and his wife a couple of times socially, but Judith wasn't the sort of person we were comfortable with. An ardent feminist, working for a homeless women's charity. Great work, I am sure, but did she need to be so challenging and dismissive of what we humble geologists were up to? John however is phlegmatic and doesn't let it worry him. He has retained some of his Hull accent and can be teased for this.

As we were coming in to land at Kano, he remarked on the way the sunlight reflected on the "derm" of the great mosque. I spent some seconds wondering what he meant until the word "dome" hit me. Back when we were students, I remember him ordering a Kirk in a pub and the lad in the bar searching the shelves for some craft beer until I told him that it was a "coke" that he wanted. The other thing about John is that, though he is not a great conversationalist, he talks to himself, or rather to the objects close to him. The tent, the augurs we were using, his boots, anything that has to be negotiated with.

Odd though it was, it has never worried me. Incidentally, John adored his feminist wife and called her his treasure. Not my style at all. My wife Alice would run a mile if I followed John's example. They have two children the same ages roughly as our two. I believe they too have just finished college, one training to be a teacher, the other a physiotherapist. Nice sensible occupations.

As to what my own accent is, I've no idea. Midland, I suppose, but modified and made anonymous over the years. No one has ever commented.

As far as I am aware, Declan is not married or even in a partnership. His university work and research on Desert Geomorphology seemed to be his whole life as far as we know. Although we did the same degree course in Geology in Britain, he moved almost straight away to California and has been there ever since. But we keep in touch and try to meet up in a professional, but at the same time, friendly way. John and I have been stuck for years in desk jobs with the same oil company, at different locations, before retirement.

During our working days, we never came in reach of anything like a pair of hiking boots, or a rock hammer. So these trips to remote places are our old boys' college reunion and a lot of fun although there is Declan's serious scientific research underpinning it.

We start by setting out a network of markers with some quick triangulation and then move across the wadi floor and the fan of sediments which gradually merged into the flat plain and the dry pan. Both the soldiers have by now become quite interested in our procedures, even though they probably don't have much idea what it is all about. What on earth is the practical use of the data we are collecting? I imagine them asking.

Occasionally, one of us would talk about sedimentation in dams in semi-desert areas, or the possibility for irrigation and crop-growing on desert margins when water supply is brought in by aqueduct or pipes, but we are clutching at straws, and it certainly doesn't impress the soldiers. This is, after all, pure research, for its own sake. We are happy with that, and the soldiers still regard the whole expedition with a sort of awe and probably suppressed ridicule. We all get on famously.

Both of the soldiers are from somewhere miles away and like their beer, unlike the cook who is devout and strictly teetotal.

On the fourth day, we wake at 5:00 am, breakfast and start to work before six. As the day wears on, clouds seem to be accumulating over the mountains, and there are sudden flurries of wind, coming funnelling down the wadi, hot blasts, followed by sudden chills. But there is little respite from the fierceness of the sun. There is an uneasy feeling in the air, and I comment on this to Declan and Philip. They both agree but just shrug their shoulders.

The sun slips in and out of the dust and cloud banks and projects strange shadows onto the desert floor and the escarpments. About midday three vehicles appear on the plain, a Mercedes and two others I can't identify. We put aside our equipment and prepare to chat, but the party ploughs on with a mere hand wave.

'Who are they?' I ask Yusuf, one of the soldiers.

He shrugs. 'Maybe Beezedo.' I try to work that one out. Ah! BZO. A mining company.

'Do they do much in this area?'

'Maybe. I can't say.'

'Perhaps you as a soldier should have stopped them and asked for their documents and permissions?'

Yusuf looks horrified. 'We are here to guard. Not investigate,' he says ruefully.

'Great,' I say, 'you're doing a good job anyhow.' I don't mean it to sound sarcastic. In the past, there have been attacks on Niger's fragile infrastructure, such as it is. Tuareg groups have only a passing loyalty to any one country and are taken up with talk of independence. There have even been abductions for political ends. But that is in the past. Here we feel no real anxiety. After all, we have two soldiers with us, haven't we?

After lunch, Gabriel asks me for the name of the next wadi south of us, closer to the mountains. We study the map together. He seems to be able to orientate himself quite quickly; perhaps he learnt that in his soldiering.

'No name,' I say.

'Anyhow that is where they go.'

'Who?'

'Those three in cars. Perhaps BZO, I watch them make the turn.'

'Well done, Gabriel. But why?'

Another shrug. 'Not good people.'

'How can you tell?'

'The way they drive and sit. And that crooked wave. Not good.'

'Well, at least they are out of our hair now.'

'What hair is that?' Gabriel asks, mystified.

I am just about to explain when there was a shout from one of the others. He is pointing across the plain. A small knot of figures, black against the reflective almost saline surface.

Gradually, they resolve into one man on horseback and two others on camels at the head of a column of several others, including women and children, all with more laden camels, a dozen goats and sheep. We are working on the north side of the wadi, but it is soon clear that the Tuareg are moving towards the southern flank. Eventually, they come to a halt and appear to be casting about for something. Then they set up camp, unloading thcir black tents. They are about a mile from our own camp, but much closer to the more precipitous spur of the escarpment.

About five o'clock by which time the sky is darker and more ominous over the distant mountains, we talk about relocating our network of boreholes ready for the next day's work, but we can't help looking across at the other encampment until, eventually, I say: 'Funny really. In the middle of this emptiness, we don't say hello.'

'Well, just at this moment, I've got a lot of data to deal with,' says Declan. 'Harry, why don't you and John go over and have a chat?'

'I suppose I might,' I say looking at John and then Yusuf and Gabriel.

'Well, you can leave me out if you don't mind. I'm knackered,' says John. The soldiers look away as if trying to remember a previous engagement.

Yusuf turns to me and shrugs. 'They might even be dangerous. Some of these people are robbers. We would need to take our weapons.' (On the other hand, the careless way our two soldiers leave their weapons lying around in their tent always surprises me.) It is difficult to feel any kind of threat from anyone, especially out in the open landscape.

For the first time without any prompting, Ahmed speaks.

'There is no danger in them. Not these. But take no weapons.'

'Go over there, Harry, and take Ahmed, but no one else, and just say hello,' says Declan, 'But don't stay too long. I don't actually like the look of those clouds. And the wind.'

As we stroll over to the other side of the wadi floor, we have to negotiate dry gullies and a litter of splintered rocks. I feel a flicker of excitement. After all, this is a face-to-face meeting with almost alien people, but on their ground.

'Would you be able to speak to them?' I ask Ahmed.

20

'Perhaps. But will they want to speak to us?'

As we approach, it is clear that we have been watched all the way across. Two men move forward; the splendour of their costumes and the cloth and trappings draped on their horses is almost intimidating. They are wearing blue veils.

'Tell him who we are, Ahmed, and say we hope our camp is not in their way.'

There is a prolonged conversation which I presume is in Hausa or Arabic. The exchange seems amicable enough though the two men are clearly on their guard. Several times they point to our stakes on the valley side.

'They would like to know what you are doing. Are we going to build a luxury hotel or a power station?' Hints of sarcasm? Surely not.

'Tell them we are scientists making measurements, no more. We won't be doing any damage. In two weeks, we will be away and will leave no marks.'

'They would still like to know what work you are doing.' I begin to try to explain to Ahmed about erosion, watershed, and deposition, and he looks glum and shakes his head. Suddenly there is another voice, and a younger man, still on horseback, emerges from the rear. 'Sedimentation,' he says in English. 'What a strange word!' placing the accent on the first syllable in a French way.

'Are you familiar with its use of that word in philosophy? If I remember from my student days: "The laying bare of our presuppositions and cultural ideas, like a huge carpet, across which we walk and discover how we shall live." But in your case, you are investigating the carpet of random eroded fragments themselves. The roles of the wind, running water, temperature change… all these need to be evaluated. Natural philosophy as the old scientists used to say.'

'That's right,' I say, unsure how to continue. (What is all this about philosophy?) The man is in his twenties and clothed even more extravagantly in rich blue and red robes, with a combined turban and loose veil; a sash crusted with jewels and a dagger at his waist. Yet somehow you know it is only for decoration, not defence.

I begin to jabber on, then pause, and start again, and it is clear from his questioning that he has no difficulty with my scientific explanations about sampling and sediments. He dismounts and then points out features on the plain; an area which we had guessed became a shallow lake when it rained. The last time was thirty years ago. Two of the great empty meanders in the lower wadi floor had been reshaped after rainstorms in the mountains.

'I'm surprised, I say to find someone so knowledgeable out here in the desert,' and then regret the condescension.

'After all,' the man says, almost laconically, 'this is my *terroir*. We Tuareg are travellers. We see and hear many things. These rocks and sand and cliffs and valleys are our everyday companions. They even speak to us. We are not ignorant savages.'

I begin to apologise, but he laughs quietly and asks how far we have come, and from where? Which university are we "envoys" for? 'I have never been to America,' he says. 'Perhaps, one day I will.'

In my turn, I ask him where he has travelled from.

'Tamanrasset,' he says, 'in the west.' And his destination? 'Oh up there, north-westwards,' with an airy wave. 'We have a village there… which we visit when we can.' I feel that he isn't going to give much away.

I gesture at the sweep of the landscape and say how impressive and beautiful it is.

'Yes,' he said after a pause. 'All this,' with a dramatic gesture, 'like some scene crafted in one stupendous creative act, immutable, outside time. Yet, at the same time, we know it is millions of years old and is never static, it changes from one second to the next, subject to the natural processes of disintegration and reduction to a sea of sand.'

'I suppose so,' I say, and he looks at me and smiles at that hint of doubt in my voice. He goes on: 'But for all our gazing at the extraordinary landscape before us, and the way it stretches to the horizon, we don't take much notice of what's underneath. Unless of course there is something there to make money out of.'

I say something about that being the way of the world.

'But that is not what you are here to investigate. You are not prospectors. You are studying that very impermanence. Yet both the creative and the destructive forces of nature can fill us with the same awe. The very impermanence can be a source of wonder.'

'I think so; we can never be quite sure how the landscape will eventually evolve,' I say, warming to the theme though in awe of the direction of our conversation. I look down at my dusty shorts and sandals and feel something of an intruder into his splendid if contradictory domain. But I am intrigued too. I want to say more. 'You can see how desert landscapes proved so attractive to the filmmakers, the sense of space and that horizon.'

'Of course,' he says. 'Your Lawrence up there in Arabia. And the Spaghetti Westerns, filmed I believe in Spain.'

He goes on. 'And the birthplace of so many religious groups, with their prophets and visions. The vastness and emptiness, the sky and the infinity of the heavens. I wonder if faith is also reinforced by an awareness of what also lies beneath. Probably not.'

We are all silent then, which is the way it should be when facing the desert, though we often don't manage it.

I have to admit that I am a sucker for a landscape especially such a vast one as this with a sweep of 180 degrees or more. On a smaller scale, we have the modesty of Britain's Malvern Hills seen from the summit of Bredon Hill, or the Western Isles from Ben Nevis, and the Mawddach Estuary from the top of Snowdon. I have in the past sketched them, just to show the way they have evolved geologically. Nothing artistic, just ink sketches. It is remarkable how little notice we take of the underlying geology of our own land.

After all, we have the current fascination with the heavens, the planets stars and galaxies, yet there is still beneath our feet the actual landscape, moulded over time. We live on and cultivate that surface, adapt it to our needs. But underneath there is a hidden world of rock in layers or molten masses which we are hardly aware of it. I suppose that many poems have been written about the beauty of the landscape and the wonder of the heavens. However, those hidden layers of rock don't seem to inspire. It is almost a negative feeling we have about such matters.

Our fascination doesn't stop at the wildness of mountain landscapes. There are even cityscapes from some high buildings or adjacent hills, the City of London from Tate

Modern's roof on the South Bank or from Hampstead Heath, or Nottingham and the Trent Valley from the castle on its sandstone rock, Edinburgh and the Firth of Forth from those surrounding crags. And for all these places, there is the business of the geology underlying it and the way that the whole surface was once set up and is now being gradually moulded and altered.

Of course, in the case of the cities, most of the geology is pretty much hidden and largely irrelevant. But here in the Massif and the wadi, the exposed sandstone and limestone strata, the flattening tops of the distant isolated hills, the night frosts, the strange awareness of the creeping expansion and contraction going on under a fierce sun and cold nights, the dew and water percolation, the constant scour of the wind, all these give life and inject a sense of slow but constant change into the scene. You look and hold your breath. Overall, that enduring sense of distance and space.

It occurs to me that this young Tuareg is probably better equipped than me to analyse or describe it. I remember once hearing a famous artist say that our sense of perspective is assisted by our hearing. We see and sense great distances with our ears as well as our eyes. So deaf people, for instance, have difficulty therefore with this sensing of deep perspectives.

I remember on the other hand my wife saying that all our senses function with an overlap. Some people make this transference, sense to sense, with great ease. Synaesthesia she called it. Certainly, the sense of distance, perspective and grandeur was more than mere seeing with your eyes. My wife by the way is a scientist too, and she also looks beneath the surface. But, in her case, it is the "geology" of the brain beneath the human skull.

I should add that such reflections are unusual for me. Even the ones I have mentioned here came sometime after our talk with the Tuareg. Geology is all about rock, heat, friction and decay. Pretty hard facts and little softness or romance about it.

The young Tuareg brings us back down to another earth, so to speak. 'By the way, there will be storms tomorrow and maybe tonight even. Make sure your tents and vehicles are properly protected. I suggest you pull back from the steeper bank of the wadi.'

We prepare to leave.

'It is getting quite late. Perhaps you and your friends would honour us with a visit tomorrow evening,' he says. 'And the soldiers too.' Who has mentioned soldiers? 'We will be staying here for a while. The weather ahead of us is deteriorating, especially in the mountains. We need to wait for what tomorrow will bring.'

We thank them and make our way back.

Once out of earshot, I say to Ahmed. 'I suppose they can read much from the clouds and the winds.'

'Certainly. But they have their mobile phones too. And laptops.'

'They don't work out here.'

'Perhaps not. But you never know with the Tuareg.'

It is almost completely dark when we reach our camp, and after a few explanations, we decide to move everything closer to the escarpment. Then we turn in, preparing for another early start. I sleep very fitfully. The words of the Tuareg, and his French accent, run through my head. Where on earth did he learn to talk like that?

During the night, the winds become quite disturbing. There are electric storms flickering and flashing but with little audible thunder. Suddenly, at around 3:00, we hear the ominous swirling of water in the wadi floor. And it seems to swell and abate in turns.

Then just before sunrise, there is a crack like an explosion, a detonation, followed by an appalling grinding sound as if the mountains themselves are being bombarded and then ground to dust. My whole body trembles, and my head spins. Sand in great waves heaps up alongside our tents and funnels through the cracks. Instinctively we hold on to the framework of the tent, pull scarves over our heads and wait.

After half an hour, the worst noise subsides. We wait another hour or so for the first real light then dig our way out of the tents. A huge dust cloud hangs over the wadi floor and obliterates the view.

'I'll just climb a bit higher and have a look,' Declan says and flounders up the wadi side. Within minutes, he comes hurtling back, shouting.

'The escarpment on the other side. It's shattered. A giant rock-fall. The wadi floor and the other side were completely covered.' We all scramble up with him to the viewing point. Before us, a scene of utter devastation. The rock-falls, and an avalanche of sandy scree covers the wadi floor and the other slope, creating a dam. Behind it, water is building up.

Wow! 'Not long before it will cut through that debris and re-establish itself,' I say. 'Terrifying and yet wonderful to actually see these processes in action. Chance of a lifetime.'

'But what about the Tuareg?' screeches John. And it is as if I have been punched in the head. I have completely forgotten about them. We gaze across at their campsite almost symmetrically opposite ours. But it is not there.

Instead great piles of debris and rock sit under circling dust and sand. Complete and final entombment. And in the noise of the storm no likely warning. I feel sick. In fact, I stand up and nearly vomit. There is a roaring inside my head. Something snaps, and I shriek a curse of filth at those rain-bearing clouds (the first, we later hear, in thirty years) and the god or gods who have chosen the desert people, not we intruders, for destruction.

Declan puts out an emergency message on the radio. I drink some water to cleanse my throat, Suddenly, I feel almost light-headed. We try to make our way across the wadi, knowing that at any time the rock dam higher up might collapse. There is not a single scrap of clothing or equipment, animal or human beings visible on the surface. We shout hoping to hear some cry, but we know it is hopeless.

Perhaps, if we had those sensors used by earthquake rescue teams, we might have detected signs of life, but how long, if at all, before such sophisticated equipment could be brought in here? We wander around the site hopelessly until Declan orders us back to our side of the wadi.

Four or five hours later, a helicopter flies in. Two army officers inspect the site and question us and the soldiers. How many Tuareg were there? Perhaps they moved on before the rockfall? We kick ourselves because, in the brief meeting, we have not asked the Tuareg for their names. The helicopter people seem to take our report rather lightly. The implication seems to be that we have imagined the whole thing, in the confusion of the night's storm.

The view across the wadi after all is not so startlingly exceptional to them. There are screes and rockfalls everywhere, chaotic, piles of stones and sand, fresh un-weathered rock faces on the escarpment above. A place where a few spindly bushes have been torn from their roots. But only a geologist would be able to recognise the evidence for a recent fall. After all, these men, policemen or soldiers, have no picture of what was here before.

I scramble for my sketchbook, but the sketch I did a few days ago seems to be missing. Whether these men would have been impressed by it is another question. Somehow their casualness seems to cast doubts into our own minds. We forget to tell them about the BZO party. They instruct us to report at Zinder before returning home and then leave.

In our discussion later, we remember that explosive sound. It had not really been like thunder. Declan sends off another report on the radio about the three vehicles we had seen and their possible destination further along the escarpment. But we couldn't say who they were, even what nationality they might have been or even what they looked like. Later, we hear that BZO disclaimed all knowledge. They have no people working in the area.

3

Harry

Our data from the wadi now being incomplete and therefore useless; we pack up our stuff and move on to another site ten miles north and start again. But there is little enthusiasm. To be honest, I am one of the main culprits here. I can't get the whole tragic incident out of my mind. It is not just the sheer horror of it.

It is as if that strange meeting and our shared admiration of the sunset and the colours on the escarpment is some kind of incomplete dream. The brief connection between two wildly unrelated groups of people, and even two cultures, has been torn apart and nullified. In the end, what has happened is inexplicable. The desert landscape, fantastic in a real sense, is all bound up with it.

Normally, we geomorphologists hardly consider this mysterious side to the object of our studies, though I for one am vaguely aware. I do have this almost unnatural affection for landscapes, especially when they are so to speak stripped down to the geology. Devastating events occur… once every million years or so, but that millionth year may be tomorrow. They get recorded on time charts and reflected in the twists and turns of strata on an exposed quarry or cliff face. But they are no more than signs.

For me, the outcome of this devastating extraordinary geological incident is still unacceptable. A kind of nonsense, a massive non sequitur. My whole mind rebels against it. It is made worse for me because there is no one accountable unless you could blame God and his manipulation of the weather.

I comment to Declan on the strangeness of the sound we had heard, like a detonation, inconsistent with a prolonged rockfall, 'I can see what you are getting at. But I don't think that some other agency, other than nature itself, is at work here. It was just the combination of storm and the exposed strata's inherent weakness.'

'But it was as if someone like had blown something up,' I protest. Declan still shakes his head, and I walk away, the idea of some other agency at work still gnawing away at me.

John follows me. 'Look Harry, it was a terrible tragedy, but we are not really involved, are we? There's nothing we can do except answer the police questions. Someone later on may identify the group. Family members… if there are any… will be found.

'Someone might even set up a memorial stone. And all this assumes they were really buried under all that stuff, and we don't know that for certain. They might have just moved on. We have no evidence, either way.'

Before we had left, I made a quick sketch of the fresh rocks in the wadi though it was difficult to make much sense of the tangle of rubble.

Strange, although those questions about the erasing of the nomads from the wadi are on my mind, there is something else that is troubling me. It is as if some other puzzle which normally could be worked out logically is now proving intractable. I can no longer rely on my own brain to work things out, and so my motivations for doing anything and making any decision are scuppered. It doesn't stop there. I work my way backwards through my whole life and find all my actions, decisions and motivations are cast into doubt.

Nothing seems to make sense. The storm and the rockfall are triggers of a displacement inside my head. I become careless about the camp routines, toy with my food, and spend too much time walking around in circles, trying to find a way to sort out things, apparently with my feet. The other two just shake their heads. Even Ahmed and the two soldiers seem to avoid me.

I do also feel a bit off-colour physically. Occasionally, my head fills with a thick congestion like catarrh. My sleep is interrupted by noises in my ears. Once when we are realigning our bore holes, I stumble and fall for no reason. Not exactly fall, but collapse, rather like a puppet when all the strings have been severed.

I'm back on my feet in a moment, and tell John off for crowding me. We eventually strike camp at the new site when Declan is able to say that we have enough though not plentiful data. But it is a miserable enterprise, and we are glad when it is done.

We return to Zinder and, then on this occasion, drive south into Nigeria, dropping off vehicles, soldiers and Ahmed outside Kano. The two soldiers are back to their cheery selves. Ahmed left us earlier in Zinder. Just for a moment he put his hand on my back in a way he had never done before and said, 'The answers will come, master, they will come.' (By the way, we forbade the use of the ubiquitous word "master", but on this occasion, it just slipped out. And I felt it was for once a sign of sensitivity.)

But as we walk towards the plane, I have the feeling that with the scientific work done, we are now intruders. I think the other two are uncomfortable too, but they seem to be able to behave normally, chat with each other and look forward to getting back home.

On the plane back looking at the yellow blur of the desert below us, I continue the review of my situation. I have always prided myself on being able to organise my thoughts in a logical way. At school, I did well, especially in the sciences, and was good at sport, especially tennis. I can't say I found art or music or drama quite so amenable. They seemed such messy subjects, their objectives never clear, the results always unpredictable.

The successful exponents seemed to be fuelled by frothy enthusiasm and blind instinct. Of course, I know that is an unfair assessment. At university, I started off studying natural sciences but then in the second year, after a cool examination of my abilities and the way I might earn a living later, switched to geology. I did love the outdoors and wild places. I had always done a lot of walking, the long-distance paths, and Alice was quite keen too.

We had all the best gear for our backs, head and feet. I was an avid collector of OS maps and could navigate with a compass. But above all there were those moments when you breasted an incline, came round the edge of a scar, or emerged from a wood to see it laid out before you. Like cutting open a book which you have not read beforc. Nearly always a stillness, a sense of stasis.

What you were looking at would not change much... perhaps the cloud pattern would be altered, the smoke cowl over a distant industrial complex might shift, and light patterns would morph. But the solid earth stayed there, only changing over millions of years as earth movements and shifts and erosion patterns dictated. And so once I had trained as a professional geologist, working with oil companies in various parts of the world, my passion above all was for the empty and arid landscapes we often visited. Even Northern Norway and Alaska had that aridity and purity.

True even in those places great earth movements things were afoot, accumulation of lava under a shield of rock, or a glacier edging down a valley to the sea, but it was usually only happening slowly, outside the time frame of our human lives. It was something rather different to the current and fashionable anxiety about melting glaciers and ice sheets and climate change.

In my fourth year at university, I met Alice. She was doing medicine. We fell in love and married one year after my graduation, two years before hers. It was a strange sort of marriage partnership, but it worked for us. Me off to various oil fields in the Middle East or Africa, and she worked ridiculous hours after graduation at a London hospital. It was quite a few years later that we had the children, Thomas and Joanne.

Alice eventually moved across into an academic path, with a special interest in the brain. She worked long hours in the laboratory, yet was still had to be the mainstay of the family. I flitted in and out as work abroad dictated. Once the children were into their teens, my work became increasingly desk-bound and more static, while Alice settled into a more permanent position in the academic world in London.

We lived an hour's journey from London from where I commuted into the oil company's offices and Alice to the university. I began to see more of my two children at the point where they became teenagers and more likely to take me less seriously. But Alice was always so much in control of things, shouldering the responsibilities of home-making with skill and ease so that I tended to sit back and not interfere. A kindly uncle figure.

And then came retirement. Quite early, the oil companies were more than generous. And now I had to make decisions about what I was going to do. I needed a plan of action, a statement of intent. Golf, long walks and going out with Alice to the theatre or concerts were not enough.

I didn't have any real interest in music or theatre or books for that matter. Fortunately, the expedition to Niger was a positive move. Only now, sitting on the plane looking down at the misty yellow sea below, can I see that my position is still unresolved, and in fact is made worse by the rockfall and those Tuareg.

I remember Alice saying, 'Retirement. Golden opportunity. To do what you really care about. You need something to engage your mind,' she said almost jokingly.

She was right, but I couldn't see what it was. Going off with Declan to the desert only put things off. I certainly can't see any clearer now. In fact, like that yellow dust down there, I am still in a complete fog.

Thomas our elder one has always been a bit of a handful, from his very early teens. Although he is clever, he failed half of his exams and went around with a dodgy crowd, so Alice told me. He scraped through his degree in law and spent one year getting articled with a firm that had a particular interest in civil liberties and human rights, but then at the end of the year, suddenly threw that in and landed an internship with a commercial bank in the city. They seemed to find his know-all manner and fashionable untidiness a recommendation. From then on, he flourished and looked set for the yuppie life in the financial world of the city.

Joanne, two years behind Thomas, was a model child by comparison and looked set to go to university to do one of the arts. But then, without telling me or her mother, she applied to do medicine at Cambridge and was taken on. There had been a lot of fuss made in the press about the inflexibility surrounding access to the universities and the narrowness of the whole arts versus science argument. Switching your options like this was rather favoured.

So the two of them found their feet, though we hardly know what Thomas does now, except that within a year or so he is earning more money than I am, and fast becoming confident to the point of arrogance. Meanwhile, Joanne beavers away at her medical studies and has had to struggle to catch up on a lot of neglected basic science and mathematics. But she never had inflated ambitions or a boisterous ego like Thomas and is steadily progressing on the route to becoming a GP. She insists that it will be in a working-class area where the needs and challenges are greater.

Alice and she have recently got on better, and Alice is able to help with her studies. There had been great swathes of science and mathematics for her to catch up on. She doesn't disguise the fact that it is really hard work for her. Yet it doesn't seem to prevent her from taking an interest in what I and Alice are doing. Thomas, by contrast, is always full of what he has been doing in the city, the latest car he has bought, and foolish things he accuses the government of doing with regard to the homeless, the unmarried mothers, the immigrants, and anyone who wasn't well off. He hardly ever enquires about what I or his mother have been working on. I'm not sure it registers with him fully that I have made a recent trip to Africa.

I am reviewing all this on the plane though I am not quite sure why. As the plane comes in to land at Heathrow, I know there were some things about myself I need to work on. Some readjustment has to be made. Some decisions have to be faced up to.

The descent is a bumpy and noisy one, with a lot of banking, and I am reminded of the grinding roar of that night in our tents, the pressure on the ears as well as nose and throat, and the devastation we saw in the morning. I realise that I am looking forward to getting home and seeing Alice again. A bath, and a glass of wine, and starting to sort out the conflicts inside my head. At the same time, I know that food and wine on their own won't be enough.

4

Alice

I drove down to Heathrow to pick Harry up. He usually was in good spirits after these shindigs. After all, he was doing what he enjoyed most. Boys' games in a way, but at least something useful. In the last years, while working with the oil company it hadn't really been his cup of tea.

As I watched the three men coming through Arrivals, I could see that although Harry had a good colour he seemed quite drawn. As if something were worrying him. John's wife, Judith was standing with me. I had met her several times socially, but I found her quite taxing; so earnest and uncompromising. Very much bound up in her own life. I suppose I was too. After the usual embraces, Declan standing there in some embarrassment, I asked Harry whether they had been okay health-wise.

'Fine,' he said. 'No problems on that score.' So some other score I thought. We all said our goodbyes there in the arrival lounge, and Harry and I made our way to the car. On the journey home, he explained how the trip had gone, nothing remarkable, but that there had been some sort of hick-up, and the need half-way through to switch locations.

I wondered if there had been a disagreement between the three of them. But so unlikely after all these years. We had a meal as soon as we got in, and then even though it was only nine o'clock he said he was going to bed because he felt whacked.

I was working all the next day. When I came home I sat down and asked him again how the trip had gone. He said he'd tell me later.

'So what have you been up to today?'

'Not much. Sorting things out. This and that.' But, when I went up to the bedroom, I could see he hadn't even properly unpacked.

'So you've got the writing up to do?' I asked.

'What writing?'

'Well, your trip. And the findings. You usually do. For your own sake.'

'Yes. Well, I shall get round to it.' A pause. 'Actually, there's something else. I'll tell you after dinner.'

So we sat and ate our gloomy meal, Harry with his head down, toying with his food which is quite untypical, and me wondering what was coming up. Must be something to do with Declan or John. Then he told me the whole story of what had happened. In his best cool reporting style. No hesitancy. But still with a note of disbelief in the whole episode.

'So you see, Alice, I can't quite get it all out of my mind.'

'It must have been awful,' I said, trying to visualise it. 'Right in front of you. And so… final.'

'That's exactly the thing I can't deal with,' he said. 'As if someone gave you something unique and then just snatched it away again. Makes you think perhaps it didn't really happen.'

'Well, I'm really sorry. For them and for you, but there's nothing you can do about it is there? So somehow you've not got to worry about it. Put it behind you. If you can.'

He looked at me glumly and nodded. Now that he's got it off his chest, I thought, he will probably deal with it. He wasn't the sort of person to make a fuss about things or even to let disappointments or setbacks hold him back for long. As he would always say, you've got to work these things out.

But, as the days went by, things didn't improve. I was at home for some of the time and watched as he sat doing nothing, just looking out of the window. He went out into the garden but when I went out later to see what he was doing he was just standing there, lawns, bushes, flower beds, edges untouched. He would apologise and say, sorry, I'll sort some of this out tomorrow. Then he would suddenly take off, without telling me, walking I don't know where. Or he would be pouring over the laptop, looking puzzled. And it wasn't geology he was looking at.

I suggested a holiday. Italy or Spain. Okay, he said about as enthusiastically as if I had suggested a shopping trip to London, one of his pet hates. I mentioned golf with some of his cronies. Still no interest.

'Well, I'm going to that conference in Manchester next week,' I told him. 'Four days. Will you be okay looking after yourself?'

'I should be. I've always managed before when you were away.'

'Well, yes, normally, I wouldn't ask. But you aren't really yourself, are you? Still distracted by the incident in the desert.'

'I'll be okay. It's only cooking here, and keeping things tidy.'

'Right. So you'll be okay on your own?'

'I've said I will. No need to fuss.'

'The trouble is that I feel I do need to fuss. You aren't settling down to anything.'

'I suppose not.'

'You're brooding. I don't want to be unkind, but as far as I can see doing nothing.'

'I have a lot to think about.'

'But you can do too much of it. Thinking. Especially about that disaster.'

'Oh, I don't think it's only the disaster I'm thinking about. It's more about what I ought to be doing with my life. You've always said that I haven't sorted out how I'm going to fill my retirement.'

'Yes, I did. So how does that connect with the disaster and your Tuaregs?'

And then it all came out in an angrier and more emotional outburst. How he couldn't deal with the way he had started on something with the nomads and then the whole thing had been struck off, the people annihilated. There had been a conversation and then silence.

There should be something that had to be worked out, thought through and brought to a conclusion. But it just hung there like a deflated balloon. It made him look at his whole life, he said, and the conclusion he had come to, all the decisions he had made. There was something missing. By this time, I was getting irritated. I couldn't see where he was coming from or going to.

'So you mean your decision to become a geologist? Our marriage? The children? All blind mistakes?'

'No, nothing like that. I suppose I must be sounding very self-centred to you. A desert sunset and some heroic figure on horseback, and I'm all astray. It's just I don't seem to be able to find any motivation.'

'Well, I accept you feel a sort of indirect responsibility. But I can't see why it should intrude into your life here in this country.'

'It was the other way round. I intruded into their lives. If we hadn't been there they might have camped on our side of the wadi and been alive to tell the tale.'

'And the rockfall might have hit you, Harold. Then where would we all be?'

Thinking about this conversation later, I noticed that he didn't mention at the time the brief bouts of sickness or dizziness which he only mentioned later. I went off to Manchester. I was worried about him, but I couldn't call a halt to my work. We were at a very critical stage as regards funding. I admit I was quite occupied with it, and found Michael's mood or whatever it was distraction. I rang him each evening and "grilled" him about what he was eating and how he had spent his day. 'I've got a lot of reading to do,' he said at one point.

'What sort of thing?' I asked. 'Le Carré?' I knew he was a great fan of spy stories, though of hardly any other fiction. 'No,' he said. 'Something else. It's a book on philosophy, by Baggini. Not technical stuff. But it makes me think.'

'Wow, Harry! Philosophy!'

'I'll explain when you come back home.'

42

I put the phone down, and then on a hunch, rang our son, Thomas, on his mobile. After the usual greetings, he asked, 'How can I help you? Want something juicy for your portfolio?'

'No seriously Thomas. I'm at a conference here in Manchester. Are you going home at some point?'

'Not on at the moment, but perhaps in a week or two. Why?'

'It's your dad. You know, the trip to Niger. There was some terrible disaster that they were witness to, and he seems to have taken it to heart in some strange way. Difficult to explain over the phone.'

'Sounds like he needs a trip to the doctor's. Some tablets.'

'Oh, you know your dad. I vaguely mentioned that to him, and he walked out of the room. Anyhow, he's not actually ill, just says he can't work things out.'

'What kind of things?'

'I can't explain. His whole life. What the purpose of it, so to speak.'

'Oh dear,' in some embarrassment. 'Would I be any help? Whenever did he take any notice of what I said? I'll see what I can do though. Weekend perhaps. I'll let you know. Got to dash. Bye, Mum.'

5

Alice

Thomas managed to get himself home to visit us, just for the long weekend. I was only just back from Manchester with problems relating to our joint project. Getting three university departments to agree on a linking-up procedure was proving difficult.

Thomas often hinted that we were lucky to see our errant successful and rather affluent son once in a while. He chattered away to me about life in the metropolis. I asked him about work and the girl he was living with at the moment, but he seemed to clam up on those subjects. Harry ambled off into the garden.

'Lots to do there?' Thomas said to me.

'Plenty. But it's not getting done.'

'I suppose he's writing up his report for Declan.'

'Not much sign of that. You see, there was an unfortunate incident, a tragic one, and your dad is preoccupied with that.'

'Okay, I'll go and have a chat with him,' and he went out into the garden. When I followed a few minutes later, Harry was looking irritated.

'It was a rockfall, Thomas,' he said. 'They have avalanches in the Alps!'

'Uhh! Same kind of thing.'

'Not at all. Anyhow, that's not the point. What I find strange,' he said to me, having given up on Thomas, 'was that they, the Tuareg, had no inkling of the disaster. With their acute sense of the desert, a sort of kinship with it if you like, you would think something would have stirred in their bones, some premonition. They even warned us to make sure our tents and vehicles were well protected because there were storms brewing. And then suddenly it's as if they had never existed there. A figment. Mirage.'

'Awful,' Thomas said. 'No trace? Well, there we are.'

'Nothing.'

'Did rescue people turn up eventually?'

'Only in a very half-hearted way. The first people who came out to investigate didn't seem to take us very seriously. Our report to them seemed to be just a travellers' tale. The rockfall proved nothing, though there was still a lot of dust around to show that it was recent. Can't really blame them though.'

'Anyhow, what's done is done. Can't take responsibility. Have to move on.'

'That's what everyone says. Your mum, Declan and John.'

'You don't have any responsibility for it.'

'Some people might say we had.'

'Well, yes, I know in a roundabout way. But not personal responsibility.'

'But that's not really the main problem I have. It's more to do with the idea of something not being brought to a satisfactory conclusion. I'm used to things being thought out or thought through. I've always planned things carefully and watched them come to fruition. You know that... probably thought to yourself... that's the old man, stuck in the mud.

'But I've had my disappointments...' and he pauses. 'I knew he was thinking of the death of his parents, then that refinery merger that was a disaster that set them all back ten years and no one took the blame. But in each of those cases he had taken the hit and come out of it wiser. But, with this one, he didn't seem to see how it could be resolved. No one in Niger wanted to know about it.'

'I suppose you could ask for more information. Set up an enquiry.'

'We've done all we could.'

'So what next?'

Harry sat and looked out of the window as if he wasn't going to reply. Eventually, it came out.

'The other main problem is myself. I know it sounds pretty selfish but what do I do now? With my own life. Is there any point in planning? Are we supposed to just let things happen because the outcomes are out of our jurisdiction? I have always preferred for things to be predictable. And suddenly that view doesn't work anymore. Even logical thought itself is unreliable. The sand is always shifting. Sorry, an awful metaphor.'

'Well, I don't think you should beat yourself up about it,' says Thomas. 'Why not look out for something you could get your teeth into? There must be a demand for geologists working on short contracts. Or something in the voluntary sector. Your organising skills would be welcomed.

'And there's golf, and watching cricket. You and Mum could come up to town. Do some shows. Have a meal out. I can show you some really fabulous places to eat.'

46

'Yes, we'll think about it,' said Harry with no enthusiasm.

On another tack, I asked if Thomas kept in touch with his sister, Joanne. She was working in a practice in St. Albans having studied in London for several years. But I knew that even when she was there in the city, they rarely met. 'You must bump into her occasionally,' I had said.

Thomas said, 'Now and then.' Later, Joanne explained that the crowd he was with was a bit too high-powered for her.

'Oh, Joanne's fine,' Thomas said eventually. 'I have a chat with her quite often.'

'Well, we shall see the both of you at Christmas, shan't we?' said Harry. 'And you must bring... I'm sorry I've forgotten her name.'

'I don't think I've mentioned it. It's Adil. She's Indian.'

And that's as far as we got. Later, Thomas told me about her. Parents incredibly rich, houses in California, Greece, somewhere on the continent. A yacht on the Med. Shipping and property interests and goodness knows what else.

I tried to imagine what they would make of us as family. Thomas had told them his dad was "in oil". He didn't say he was a comparatively humble geologist. After all, Harry was in real contact with the stuff, or the actual earth from where it came. But no "oil-man" in the Texan mould. I probably could cope with that family but Harry would flounder.

On the Monday morning, Thomas took the early train back to London.

6

Harry

I have an idea buzzing around in my head; a return trip to Niger. I phoned Declan to see if there is any more work to be done there.

'To do what?'

'Well, you know, more measurements, observations to support... what we've already done.'

'Are you sure that's what you mean? Or are you also still chasing up those Tuareg?'

'Well, I could look into that too if I had some spare time.'

'You don't kid me, Harry. I can't honestly think of anything we really need. But I'll get back to you.'

He phones the next day to say that I am in luck; there is a package on its way. He has satellite photos of an area in the south of the country which requires ground data, photos and sketches. Two or three days work at most. What I do with my spare time is not his concern.

Once I get the package I talk to Alice. I explain how vital the work is that has been assigned to me by Declan, and she smiles sweetly, and says, 'What else? You going after those Tuareg?'

'No chance. This work is in the south, nowhere near the wadi and the Tenere. But I may be able to pick up some information.'

'Perhaps I should come with you? You know I've never visited s desert.'

'Great. But can you afford to be away at this point?'

'No. I really can't. Cambridge is being really awkward. I have to see it through. You go, get your samples and things and see what you can find out about your blessed Tuaregs. Whatever happens, it will help put your mind to rest.'

So I make preparations. Visas, flights, hotel, a car and driver. Meanwhile, Alice is back in Cambridge. I hope she meets people with whom she can have a civilised conversation. Her husband is no candidate for that.

The flights to Niger are complicated. First Paris, then Niamey, the Niger capital, then the short hop to Zinder where I pick up my car and driver. After dropping things off at my hotel, we drive for two hours to our site on Djouba Road. It's not dramatic mountain scenery, just a low ridge covered with sparse vegetation. I am to collect samples which will demonstrate soils affected by increasing drought in the area... a long-term climate change.

After a couple of hours of sampling, the driver and I climb a low pile of rocks. Beneath we can see a circle of cattle and people round a well. We clamber down and watch. Two groups of women, muscular shoulders bared, are hauling on ropes and drawing up water in great leather buckets. There seems to be a great deal of ribbing and laughter.

I wave my camera at them, asking for permission to shoot, and they laugh some more and strike poses which is the last thing I want. But I get one or two good shots in between. One group are dressed in colourful clothing, the other in black. I ask the driver to ask if they are Tuareg. He shakes his head, and I have to be satisfied with that.

We go back to our vehicle and return to Zinder and the hotel. The driver will pick me up the next morning, and we will call the police to ask for information about the Tuareg. The hotel is a dreary empty place, and I watch some dreadful TV, manage to speak to Alice briefly, and then go off to bed.

The next morning, I have a frustrating interview with a police official. They are hardly aware of the rockfall incident and presume that it has all been consigned to the files. No, there is no one they can suggest that I might consult, no official representative of the Tuareg. For that, I would have to go to the capital.

I leave empty-handed and ride out along the Djouba Road to complete my scientific work. There is a sort of harmattan mist which drains all character from the landscape. When I eventually get back to the hotel there is a message for me. A representative of the French embassy would like to speak to me and will be at the hotel at five.

The representative is a young woman, Steffi Lacombe, light-skinned, very short but compact build with a business-like air. Quick movements, Good English with a trace of a French accent. She explains that my name has been given to them by the police and that I am looking for information about the Tuareg.

'I can't provide you with anything directly. It's not our role out here. But I might know something which will help. Tell me about the whole thing. I need your first-hand account.'

So, over a cold beer, I tell her the whole story. Our journey, my friends, The soldiers and the cook, the research we were doing, the wadi location, the meeting with the Tuareg and the storm and rockfall. I am encouraged by her apparent real interest and go on to describe my conversations with the Tuareg. Our curtailed philosophical debate in the sands.

When I have finished, she doesn't say anything but just sits there thinking. I feel a bit uncomfortable. But then she apologises. 'Sorry, another train of thought. But it may prove a relevant one. I can see that the experience has moved you. As it would anyone. Now, like you, I've made enquiries, but those have drawn a blank.

'But there is something in the back of my mind that is sending out signals. Bear with me. I trained as a lawyer in the capital. There was a student in our year who called himself Nik, but that wasn't his real name. He was by far the most brilliant in our year, and also he was gorgeous.

'He was studying philosophy as well as law and was awarded a scholarship to the Sorbonne. But this is the point. He returned from Paris. We assumed he would become a diplomat or whatever, but he suddenly disappeared into the desert. No one knew quite where.

'The Tuareg don't post their whereabouts online, and of course, there are some groups that are subversive, have terrorist links and talk of self-determination. That's why I can't afford to appear to be too interested. But from what you have described, I think he may be your man.'

'Yes. He did comment on our use of that word, Sedimentation, but in some philosophical context which I didn't really understand.'

'I'm afraid that's all I can tell you. I will keep my eyes and ears open, but I don't really anticipate there will be more.'

'And was his name really Nik,' I say.

'No, I think his real Tuareg name was Umar.'

I thank Steffi for her story. I'm convinced that it is the same man. It helps me to give him a clear identity. The person I had inside my head had been slowly evaporating in the heat. I was even suspecting that I had imagined him and our conversation.

I asked Steffi if she would share a meal with me. She says that regretfully she has a prior commitment, a tedious official one that she cannot avoid. In any case, she indicates that the food in my hotel is notoriously poor. She can recommend somewhere much better. Perhaps, in the next few days, she can arrange something.

Rather foolishly, I say, 'You're right. The food here isn't brilliant. You, being French, would find it awful.' But then I stopped myself. 'Sorry, I'm making assumptions…'

'It's okay. My father was a French engineer, my mother is Hausa. He returned to France and the marriage broke down. But we have always been well provided for, hence my education. I shall advance in the service and may even get to Paris. I am clearly not much of a catch for marriage to diplomats or the businessmen I meet. I think that helps me to do my job better.'

'In the circumstances, you have been more than helpful. I'm sure those people you mention are missing a trick if you pardon the expression.'

She laughed. 'I've never been called a trick before.'

I blushed. 'I didn't mean it like that. It's just a silly English expression. I'm sure you will have lots of opportunities ahead of you, of all kinds. Is that more diplomatic?'

'I'll go away with that. I will need it for this event tonight. Have a good stay, and I hope you get your scientific work done successfully. I'll be in touch if anything else comes up.' We exchanged addresses and phone numbers, and she wrote the name of the restaurant where the food was "tolerable" and then with a wave she walked rapidly to her jeep. The speed at which she departed turned a few heads.

7

Harry

Although I am tempted by the good food of Steffi's recommendation, I have too much on my mind and manage with mediocre food at the hotel. I stroll around the main square and streets after the meal, but can't see any Tuareg. Usual cacophony of vehicles and people with hand barrows and occasionally sheep and goats.

I return to my room and ignore the television. I speak briefly to Alice, and we joke about my meeting with glamorous attaches from the French embassy. Silly really, because Steffi had been such good and lively company. I wish Alice had been there with me.

At eight o'clock, there is a message for me. Steffi will be there in an hour. New development. We meet in the hotel lounge. Steffi is almost breathless. Real coincidence. We had a family arriving last night from Nigeria. Claim they may be your Tuareg's parents.

The hotel here has a private VIP room we can use. Okay. There will be a government official there too. I'll stay as long as I can. You may find the family difficult... not in any aggressive way, just awkward. They have lived in Nigeria for two generations.

When Mr and Mrs Muhammed arrive, they are in Nigerian dress, and we greet each other quite formally. They seem quite wary. Over drinks, I tell them the whole story. How the party appeared on the horizon, how we went across to speak to them, our return to our own camp, and the invitation to visit them the next day.

Of the discussion, I had with their son I say nothing. Then as briefly and unemotionally as possible, I tell them of the storm in the night, the filling up of the wadi, and the rockfall. The next day, absence of any evidence on the surface that they had even been there. They both listen impassively, but I notice that the man is beginning to become impatient. I get the impression too that there is no doubt in their minds that it was their son.

Mr Muhammed sits as if summoning his thoughts. He seems angry, but with whom? Then it comes out.

'Why he go there? These empty places. There's nothing there. A bloody waste place. Why he go?'

Steffi answers: 'Perhaps he is trying to discover something about his roots,' she says, but the word sounds like a cliche. 'Some kind of authenticity. Or freedom.' Both words seem a bit daring to me. Mr Muhammed clearly doesn't like them.

'Roots? What are roots? What kind of freedom? Here in Nigeria,' with a hand sweep vaguely southwards, 'he could have whatever he wanted. We gave him the best. He is a good scholar and goes even to Europe for more schooling. By now, he could be diplomat or politician down there in Abuja. Or he could join me in my business. So much opportunity. Bloody wasted.'

And he shakes his head in despair. It occurs to me that he is speaking as if his son is still alive. Chastising him for not conforming to what they were expecting him to deliver. I ask how long it has been since they made contact with him.

He sends message every few month. From where we don't know. Last time was four months ago. Then someone tells us that people are asking questions, trying to locate someone and his band of followers. So we make enquiry too, through our government. 'What name he give?'

'I'm sorry. I didn't get around to asking. Silly of me. He was most kind and invited us to go and see them the following evening. Sadly…'

'The name Umar has come up,' says Steffi.

'Yes, that is what he calls himself,' said the man gloomily. Then he adds: 'Is he joining with those rebels in the desert? Bad people?'

'Well, they didn't seem to have any weapons,' I say. 'Just the dagger as if for decoration.'

Suddenly the mother speaks. 'He always do what he want,' she says and holds her hands up above her head in despair. Then out of the blue, she asks me: 'What he look like?'

I struggle to describe his costume and his voice… an educated one I stress.

'But his face?'

'I'm sorry, but he was wearing a veil wasn't he.'

She nods and again throws up her hands. I feel I have to say something more.

'He looked very fit. He was kind to us and wanted to help. He spoke as if he was… Well, I suppose, content with the life he was living. I would have liked to speak with him more. We only had a few minutes.'

And at last a smile and a hint of a sideways glance at her husband. As if a morsel of comfort has been taken to her mother's breast. Perhaps a veiled defiance at her husband's obstinacy. I enquire from Mr Muhammed whether they plan to visit the site of the rockfall.

'Why we go there?' He doesn't seem to expect an answer. He speaks to the blue-suited official, who tries to look as if he too is searching for an answer. 'With current unrest situation most unwise. What can we hope to find?' he says in strained English.

'Why we go there?' the man continues angrily. 'Endanger our lives? To put up a memorial stone? The proper place for his body is with his family in Nigeria. My father is buried there, many uncles, brothers.'

Again the woman speaks. 'But if we go there, how will we go?' The official shakes his head and indicates I suppose that it would be no mere journey. An expedition would have to be mounted.

Mr Muhammed adds, 'How do we recover corpses? We dig? Perhaps they are not there under the stones. Now in Khartoum drinking tea,' he says with a cheery grin.

And that seems to be it. We shake hands again formally. The handshake from the mother is warmer, and I have a glimpse of something like gratitude. But not from the man. Perhaps he thinks that for me a trip to Niger is not such a great thing. Just to listen to his complaints about his son's decision to return to the nomadic life.

When they have gone, I thank the official, whose name I forget, for arranging the meeting, and he departs.

'You can see that it is difficult. I'm not sure what his parents want us to do,' says Steffi. 'They had already lost him. It's as if in a way he was no longer their son.'

'But I think the mother still feels the loss,' I say. 'You know in a more personal way.' With that, Steffi says she has to get on and says she's sorry that the meeting with the Muhammeds hasn't been any help. She would let me know of any other developments.

The next morning, waiting for the midday plane, I had another look at the maps. The strange pencil red line drawn across the escarpment area has the letters Ver…ung alongside it, with the middle letters rubbed out. It's German I presume. Will have to find out what it means.

At one point, I doze off and in a short dream, Ver…ung is revealed as a war with tanks, guns and rocket launchers. It is not clear whose side I am on in this war. But the soldiers in the tanks and behind the weapons are all Tuareg. One of the camels looks strangely like Mr Muhammed.

8
Harry

I return to England with nothing resolved in my mind. When I explain this to Alice she is kind enough not to say, well, I told you so. She has had her disappointment; the three varsity link-up has not worked out. Cambridge is out of the picture for various reasons. Feelers are being extended to Birmingham.

But there are a lot of phone calls again, and I wonder miserably whether there are other people she feels she can talk to, rather than her disengaged husband. I pray fervently that they are not male. For no good reason. My preoccupations are not good for either of us. It is as if each of us has our own problems to deal with. My strained state of mind merely confuses her attempts to bring three organisations into step. And vice versa.

Eventually, I sit down to write the report on our trip to Niger. And that is when I discover something that really made me sit up. That geological map of Niger with the mysterious red line. The German dictionary soon reveals the likely word; Verwerfung. Fault line.

One of those surface discontinuities is usually caused by lateral or vertical movement of the strata millions of years ago. It takes a practised eye to pick one out in the landscape unless you have a detailed geological map in front of you. The desert maps we have are grossly oversimplified. This red line runs close to the edge of the escarpment and links our wadi with that one close by where the people we thought might be BZO were encamped. The unreliable but persistent notion bounces around in my head that the detonation we seemed to hear at the beginning of the rockfall was man-made.

Perhaps they used explosives to investigate the rocks close to the fault line. The disturbance might have been sufficient to trigger the dramatic collapse of the unstable escarpment at our wadi. I mean, why would someone set off an explosion at night? Answer: to disguise it, especially at the height of a storm when all hell, weather-wise, is being let loose. In my own mind, I already have BZO in the dock; but the case against them is very flimsy.

I write all this down, including the conversation with Mr and Mrs Muhammed and append it to my geological report to Declan. A nice letter back, thanks for all the data, and one or two of my excellent sketches, but much as he would have liked to have someone to blame for the rockfall, everything that happened that night has for him the hallmarks of a natural disaster. No human agency is required.

There is no real evidence that BZO were present or that they were using explosives. The fault line would be unlikely to be active or that sensitive. He understood that I was eager to find some explanation for the death of the Tuaregs, but he didn't think I was going to get anywhere with it. The geomorphology we knew made the rockfall a "natural" occurrence, however tragic had been the result.

'Come on, Harry,' he says later on the phone. 'You saw those officials in Niger... at no point did they seem anxious or interested. Your second visit seems to confirm that. Even his parents are not interested.

'I'm sure that BZO will have a hand in many a dirty business. But not in Niger. Only a massive operation with experts and the army would be capable of revealing more. But that's not going to happen. I'm sorry, but I do have to be blunt.'

And I know in my heart of hearts he is right. And as everyone seems to be saying, whatever you do, whoever is blamed, it won't bring the Tuareg back. And yet there is something or somebody inside me that is still hoping for something to come to light.

I decide to distract myself from it all by having a good look at all my own sketches and putting them into some sort of order. There is also the laborious task of converting the best ones to ink. If I do go any further with this, I will have to decide how to present them. Perhaps I could select the best ones... not only the ones from Niger, but others from Britain and abroad... and mount them into a large loose-leafed folder. With proper annotations and descriptive notes, not scribbles. There are some days when I feel practically euphoric about this. But it doesn't last. I can't seem to see the point of it.

Alice is commuting to London and during the day the house feels empty. The weather is windy and wet, and my walks are short ones. And the Niger disaster along with my overall view of retirement still hovers like a mirage that won't go away.

However, a second metaphorical rockfall comes even before Alice returns from a two-day visit to Manchester. It threatens to knock me further off my balance. And its chief cause is Thomas.

A couple of weeks earlier, Thomas made a flying day visit in his Porsche Boxer or was it Boxter? Or even Poxter? He was unusually ill at ease, although still inviting Alice and me to taste the delights of food and entertainment in the metropolis. After all, he said, you Mum are going up there for work without enjoying any leisure time there. I've never myself got a handle on what "leisure time" really meant.

When I asked him about work, he was evasive and probably as unforthcoming as I was, but I couldn't be bothered to interrogate him further. It was a relief to see him roar away in the gilded chariot of his ill-gotten gains. But he still seemed preoccupied with something.

Three days later, I get a call from him, 'Could I pick him up that evening at the station at 6:15? Yes, that evening.' Alice is due back at 9:00 pm from London. I retrieve three meals from the freezer.

At the station, Thomas is cheery, but I can detect stress underneath.

'No car,' I say in a jocular way.

'I'll explain about that later.'

Once we are home I heat two meals under the microwave and open a bottle of wine. We eat without much talk except about the weather and the latest phone message from Alice. Washing up is done in no time while Thomas sits looking out of the window at nothing in particular. Is he preparing some kind of speech?

Then it all comes out. I realise that I may not be getting the full and awful story. He has been asked to resign. It is either that or something worse. He meant to tell me earlier but couldn't summon the courage.

Some kind of investigation. All very unfair. He and a couple of others have been working on a scheme involving the purchase and sale of shares. It was all going along fine, even if it was tricky to handle. They didn't get an endorsement from the office (The bastards!) because they knew it was outside their comfort zone.

In a sense, they were happy turning a blind eye. They (who were "they", I wanted to ask, but it didn't seem the right time) were always saying how they admired initiative. Then, suddenly, out of the blue, some watchdog people (cunning, conniving, bald-headed desk-men!) have started ferreting about, and begin to talk about compliance and irregularities. The next minute the cretins raise questions of legality.

'Are you saying that the whole thing was a scam?' I ask.

'Nooo. Not really. I mean the word scam can be interpreted in various ways, can't it.'

'Don't ask me. Scams for me are set up by crooks. Little old ladies lose half of their savings. They are just careless or dim-witted, I suppose?'

'That's not fair, Dad. The people who were to lose in this affair were well-heeled.'

The firm has made him and his friends an offer. Resign or let the investigation go ahead with the possibility of criminal proceedings. No one in the firm would be likely to spring to their defence. Anyhow, in some ways, he is glad to be out of it. And yes, it was a risky venture, and on second thoughts, it wasn't quite kosher. But you learn from your mistakes, don't you?

'Do *you*?' I ask as sweetly as I can.

'Probably yes. But don't rub it in.'

'So what happens now?'

'Nothing much. I will have to move out of the flat. The car will have to go back. There's a good market for used Porsche's. Then look for another job.'

'In the city?'

Thomas pulls a face. 'Once you blot your copybook, the word soon gets round. They make sure it does. It annoys me so much... they don't care whether what you have done is illegal or not. If it works, they enjoy the credit, if it goes awry they get on their moral high-horses.' There was a pause. 'The way I'm explaining all this sounds like a novel... blots, copybooks, horses. Perhaps that's what I should have gone for.'

Neither of us speaks for several minutes. Should I be consoling or accusing? It was clear that Thomas knows what he has done, in his own offhand way, and is making for my sake some admission of guilt.

'So do you feel in the long run that you will be able to put this behind you?'

'I'll have to.'

'And where will you live?'

'Well, that depends on where the work is. Would it be okay for me to come home just for a few days until I sort out a job?'

'Fine. Plenty of room here. You will have to talk about this with your mother though. She'll be here at any time.'

'Actually, I went to see her earlier today. That's why I didn't get here till 6.'

'What in London? But she would have been busy. That scheme they are working on is going through a bad patch.'

'Yes, I realised when I met her. But I managed to speak to her for a few minutes.'

'She would have been delighted to see you there, I'm sure. And with such cheering news!'

She was livid. Not like you. We were in a sort of annexe, but I think other people could hear. She shouted at me about disgracing the family name and all that. 'Your father will be mortified,' she said. 'We'll talk about it later tonight when I get home.'

'What a mess! Do you know your mother is at a very critical stage with her funding bid? If news of this got out, I can imagine that she would be too embarrassed to proceed.'

'Yes. For that, I would be solely to blame,' he says crestfallen. 'But I don't think any more will come out. Those bastards have too much to lose.'

That still sounded like someone angling for someone else to blame.

'Dad, that bit about you being mortified. Are you?'

'In a sense, yes. I don't know what to say. Your mother is better at nailing things down. In matters of money, there are no grey areas. And I agree wholeheartedly. But the one thing that concerns me is, how are you going to put things right?'

'It can't be put right. Just pushed away and forgotten.'

'I wasn't thinking in terms of putting the clock back, but of you straightening your life out. With this black mark against your name?'

'Dad, this isn't proven fraud. I'm not a crook. It isn't going to go to court.'

'You said yourself that word gets around.'

We sit in silence, each following a train of thought 'But you're just condemning the scheme, Dad? You've not mentioned disgrace.'

'Perhaps I should. But it's what you do next that seems to be most important. Fraud on any scale or of any complexion is fraud. Perhaps I'm not very good at showing my approval or disapproval. But I think you've let yourself down. There are times when you can take risks, but in the end, you've got to toe the line. For the sake of your own conscience above all. Aren't there people in the financial world who will employ you, even if it is on a lower scale?'

'Only ones that might connive at what we did. People to avoid. People who would say, next time cover your tracks, don't get caught, those sorts of people. No, it's going to have to be a complete change of track. Do geologists employ unqualified apprentices? I could cart round bits of equipment?'

I tell him that it is not likely. 'You might look into some sort of course which provides training. Say in management or teaching. After all, you have a degree in law.'

'Yes, I've been thinking about that. But it would probably be expensive.'

'Well, that's where I could help. I mean I do have some investments you know. Nothing very glamorous, as you didn't hesitate to infer last time we looked at the portfolio But enough to finance you for a year or two.'

Thomas looked at me curiously. 'The Prodigal Son? Given another chance?'

'The parallel is not a good one. Even if you were feeding pigs there in the city. And your sister is not the one who stayed loyally at home. And there would be no feasting. No, you

66

would have to be looking at courses that led to sensible and legal employment.'

'Thanks, Dad. I'm not sure that I deserve it. Let me think about it, look into it, and then tell you what my options are.'

'But what I've said still needs to be cleared with Alice. She may say, there's the door! Go and stew in your own yuppie juice.'

'That would be fair enough,' he says.

'Can I ask about your girlfriend?'

'Oh, that's all over. Adil was not so very upset, but her parents were speechless. They didn't tell me to sling my hook. But it was clear that I was expected to be on my way. Adil was upset about our break-up but not devastated. I may still see her around.

'Or perhaps I won't. I'm not likely to bump into her. They really do live in another world, and I don't have access to it any longer.'

That evening it is half past nine before Alice gets back.

'A good conference?' I ask.

'Yes and no. We managed to set up the three-way link with Birmingham now on board. In spite of me having to listen to a tale of fraud, deception and woe during the coffee break. All of which I'm unwilling to discuss this evening. I'm too tired, satisfied with one outcome, and appalled by the other. Tomorrow we discuss. At 9:00 am. If that's convenient for you both?' And she goes off to bed without another word.

During the night, I wake up twice, jerked into consciousness by some weird dreams and a sense of guilt. For a moment, I couldn't think what the cause was. Then I remembered: Thomas's backsliding might be just as devastating as the Niger disaster. What if it stuck to him like a burr whatever job he got? And then my mind leaps further back, where had Alice and I gone wrong in his upbringing.

Had we encouraged him in his recklessness? Anger mounts in my head. Were we being too forgiving for Thomas's good? I sit up and try to read but the book about spies in Turkey only irritates me. 'Go back to sleep,' mumbles Alice, and I get some comfort from clasping her while she falls off to sleep.

The next morning, we go over all the ground and Thomas's options. Thomas is very submissive. But what else could he be? If his mother pointed to the door, I would go along with that. It is to his mother that Thomas looks when it comes to the crunch. I think he is even a bit scared of her. That bit of fear might be the thing that puts his back on the right track.

Alice asks him about money. Would he be able to support himself without assistance? Would he be able to finance retraining? He says yes, to some extent. I repeat my offer of limited funds. But I have to wonder about any money he has, how was it obtained, was it "tainted" so to speak?

I keep that thought to myself. We talk about two options: teaching, or back to the law again, if they will have him. Otherwise, it will be some sort of administrative work. Just the kind of thing he would hate.

Thomas says can he have a few days to think about it all. Or even just one day. And we agree that is the best way to proceed. He dashes back to London to sort out the sale of the flat and car and is back the next day with most of his other stuff. I've spoken to Alice in the meantime.

'Do you think I'm being too generous with that offer about money for retraining?'

'Not at all, dear. But we don't want to make it too easy for him, do we? Keep him in suspense. He has his resilience. Time to give it a test.' She doesn't seem to be in the mood for discussion.

'Anyhow, great that you've got the three universities working together. The funding ought to be easier to obtain.'

'Well, we'll see. The funding is secure. We're just waiting for the official approval. Anytime. Sorry, I didn't tell you earlier. Mixed feelings about Thomas.'

'So there's cause for celebration.'

'Not yet. Even though this guy said it was a certainty, I'd prefer to wait for the official letter. In the meantime, how have you been?'

'Strange. This business with Thomas is like a bad dream turned into reality. To some extent, it has pushed all that Niger stuff into the back of my mind. Just for the moment.'

'But not dismissed it?'

'I suppose not.' I tell her about Declan's reply to my report and that fault line. Nothing really new there.

9

Harry

After Thomas's departure, Alice and I discuss the Thomas situation again, while waiting for him to reveal his intentions. 'He needs to get a grip on himself,' says Alice. 'Look for something straightforward. No frills or glamour. Make a proper job of it.'

After a pause, she says: 'Don't I sound prissy and awful?' We are sitting in the garden with our coffee even though the weather is not very inviting. She adds, more reflectively, the same thoughts that I have been having. 'I suppose we should have been more attentive. Not allowing him so much freedom with his wildness. But he seemed to be doing so well, up there in the city. So confident about it. It all still makes me very angry.'

We discuss those new avenues of training. But some, like teaching, for instance, don't quite seem to be ones for Thomas.

'There's the civil service. Or local government. Social services.'

'That might be quite expensive,' Alice warned.

'Well, surely, he will have some money. Once he's sold that Porsche. And I've said we'll help out.'

'Yes, but can we trust him to be sensible and not fritter that away on some hair-brain scheme.'

'Well, I think he may have learnt his lesson.'

'You're being very kind to him. He's let himself and us down badly. I feel awful about the extent we may be involved in this fraud. He tells, me that all my investments are "kosher". Even that word makes me cringe. Sound, secure and legal are the words I would prefer.'

'Still, we have to look on the positive side. He is making the effort, looking for a way to…'

'Go straight?' With a snort. 'Where do these sorts of words come from?'

In the end, we agree that he should be encouraged to look into all the possibilities. Although we leave it at that, it is going to be all up to what Thomas comes up with.

A week later, Joanne is here for a short stay. The practice in St. Albans where she works takes up all her time and energy. Yet I always feel at ease with Joanne even though we are don't often agree on political issues. She is wearing the usual rather too-large and baggy sweater and jeans, her hair tied up on top of her head which makes her look taller.

As always, there is no pretence with her, no complaints about the people she works with, nor the administration of the practice. But it is long hours and some stress. She sees people and knows what treatment is best for them, but it probably isn't available on the NHS. A lot of people get second best along with long waiting lists.

We are out in the garden again, the three of us. The neglect of the garden is manifest though no one comments. Thomas has apparently told Joanne the bare outline of his city debacle incident, so I fill in a few more of the details, and she listens without comment. I tell her that I detect a glimmer of regret, even guilt, in her brother, in spite of his usual display of contempt for the firm that had sacked him. I tell her about him losing his smart flat, girlfriend and Porsche.

'Oh dear. He will miss those. But he always liked taking risks, even dragging me into it when we were little.'

'But surely common sense, or something about honesty, should have told him he was going too far this time. We feel that we should have been more aware. Prepared to warn.'

'And would he have taken much notice? I don't think so. Perhaps this is a better way to get a warning. So what will he do next? Another city job?'

'He says no. The word will have gone round and doors will be closed.'

'Well. that's a good thing too. He needs to make a completely fresh start. He should go back to college.'

'That's what your mum and I have told him. I think he's taking it all quite seriously and looking into it. In his own idiosyncratic way. What do you think he should go for? It has to be something which has nothing to do with money.'

'You know he never worked very hard at school and mostly got good results. If he's determined, I don't think he would find a new avenue of study difficult. As long as he sticks with it. Of course, it's not for me to say. Funny, isn't it? When I said I wanted to switch from English to medicine, neither Mum nor you were keen. And now we are trying to think of ways of switching David's career path.'

'Did we try to discourage you?'

'Oh yes. Not in so many words. Gloomy looks.'

'Well, that just shows how little we knew.'

On Sunday, Alice suggests the woodland walk. The three of us. Something we haven't done for ages. The track is muddy but Joanne says her trainers will be okay, and she has spare shoes in the car. Leaves are just beginning to pile up, and the wheat and barley fields are bare or covered in stubble.

On the horizon, the Pennines are just visible. I tell Joanne again the whole story of the wadi even though she has heard it briefly before. Alice listens attentively; surely it must either bore her or irritate her. I wonder if it is all beginning to sound tedious. An old man preoccupied with what was surely only a transitory experience. Something without an outcome.

'And you didn't find out anything more on your second trip?' says Joanne.

'Absolutely nothing. A complete waste of time. That's what everybody told me before I went.'

'But let's get this right,' Alice buts in. 'It wasn't so much that you thought going a second time would sort out the mystery of the rockfall. You wanted to go, in order to rule a line under the whole chain of thought and uncertainty that these Tuaregs have opened up for you. But it isn't settled for you at all, is it? Not yet.'

'I don't think so. I suppose Thomas's antics have temporarily shifted the spotlights. But there we are. It's what you've told me before. Clear-cut conclusions cannot be relied on in any walk of life when you need them. And I'm not good with loose ends.'

'Perhaps,' says Alice, 'that's been your strength throughout your whole life so far: thinking things through, getting it all clear and then acting on it. Whereas here you are faced with the ultimate loose end. One that won't allow itself to be sorted. There is no "end" to the thread. It will always be there…'

'I'm not sure this loose-end theory isn't getting out of hand,' I complain.

We have got to the corner of the wood. The path disappears into a long forest drive that will bring us back home. An owl flies over the path, close enough for us to see the discs of his eyes. 'Now, there's someone who is clear-sighted. Wisdom on the wing,' I say.

'I doubt it,' says Alice. 'He may be wise in his own way, but I suspect he has what we might call a one-track mind. The problem we have with you Harry stems from your two-track mind… left and right side brain out of balance. I'm going to have to give you a lecture on it.'

'My god. Not the dreaded scalpel. A lecture on what?'

'The brain. Your brain, Joanne's, Thomas's, mine.'

'It will make a nice after-dinner entertainment. Instead of charades.'

'I might opt out of it,' says Joanne. 'I'd like to have an early night. I've got so much on next week.'

After the meal and a chat together, Joanne goes off to bed. Alice and I are left in a sort of stalemate. I'm not sure what is simmering between us.

'Okay,' I say. 'Lecture begins. Do you want to strike a pose? You stand there by the fireplace, while I cringe at your feet.'

'No, Harry. Let's just stay as we are. This isn't a lecture. It's just telling you where I am with this research. I think it might be of some help to you. But no lecture.'

She takes a deep breath. 'First. To sort of clear the ground. Would I be right to make some assumptions about you? Being thorough and conscientious in all you do is important, isn't it? The detail and the way it is logically organised in your head matters whether it is some rocks, a map or a bus timetable.

'It's the same with the way you look after me and the family. I know it was difficult when you were travelling with work, but you were never neglectful. If something wasn't working out in the family, you and I were able to think it through and find some sort of answer. Sometimes you over-thought things, pursuing quite mundane things to a mercilessly logical conclusion. You allowed logic to override what I thought was more instinctive. Common sense.'

'You may be right. I do like to analyse things like that. I'm sure it is a fault especially if it means I ignore someone who's talking good sense.'

'I'm not saying that the path of logic isn't a good one. The best one in most circumstances. But there has to be something else. This Niger business needs something more. First of all, there's no reason why you should feel guilty.

'In some grand overarching view of the world, of course, we feel some guilt when people suffer. Earthquakes, Tsunami, Famine. We sympathise and wonder why we haven't devised ways of side-lining these natural disasters. But scientific research has a long way to go. One day they may be able to predict the location and timing of earthquakes and people's lives may be saved.

'But I guess it's a long way to go. Here today, with your rockfall, we have something that may prove insoluble. Oddly, you John and Declan are actually studying it, for purely academic reasons. You might even venture to make predictions about it. But it caught you on the hop.'

'You can't call what we do predictive. Just vague guesses in the broadest possible terms. The occurrence of rainstorms in the tropics, the fragile nature of those wadi sides. All terribly inexact. Could happen tomorrow or in a hundred years' time.'

'Maybe. So all the more reason for saying that your feeling of guilt is misplaced. In fact, dare I say it, illogical!'

'You're right. Logically I am free of blame. But that doesn't stop me from "feeling" guilty about the outcome of the rockfall. And about not being able to complete that conversation with the Tuareg. And then we have all this quite unrelated trouble with Thomas.'

'Of course. It's natural you should feel that about Thomas. Me too. We're looking at the whole picture of his upbringing. Not just his wild teenage years. Inevitably, you feel there may have been inconsistencies. But doesn't every parent fall short somewhere? To bestow a perfect upbringing on your offspring is impossible. Another "illogical".'

Suddenly there is movement at the door. 'Sorry. Couldn't help hearing what you were saying. I couldn't sleep anyhow.'

'Come in and join in the fun,' I say and make room for her on the settee.

'It needs to be said,' says Joanne, 'that we two had a lovely life. At some point, you, Dad, are thinking, "Oh, I wasn't there for them", but that's all nonsense. It's what you are as a whole over the years of childhood and adolescence that matters. Not what happens at some single point. So what Thomas did in London was his sole responsibility. Your two events, Thomas's affair and the rockfall aren't really connected at all.'

'And,' says Alice, 'you need to use both sides of the brain to deal with them. They don't match. You need different viewpoints to address each one. Your left side is capable of that, but not your right.'

'Mum's right,' says Joanne.

'Oh dear,' I say. 'Now, two doctors on the case. Help.'

Immediately Joanne is contrite. 'I didn't mean to interfere, Dad. It just seems to be a way of looking at it all. After all, I'm only a GP apprentice. What do I know about how the brain works?'

'The point is this,' says Alice. 'It is precisely that common sense way of thinking about the brain that is a characteristic of the left side. Just what a good GP needs too. I can see that I will have to watch myself when I get into lectures on behaviour. Theories, charts and data may be very well. A first-hand experience of "normal" people might be a better starting point.'

'Oh, Mum, if you only knew how piecemeal my knowledge is at present. Someone comes in with a cough. There are a dozen avenues to investigate, quite apart from peering down their throat.'

'That's where experience not data will make all the difference. You're making a good start anyway. Me, a scientist investigating the brain! Faced with an unexplained headache I wouldn't know where to start.'

On a different tack, Alice asks: 'What was it your Tuareg said about the permanence and change in the desert landscape?'

'Wow! You've remembered that well. Yes, he used a French word, Sedimentation, for it. We use the word in geomorphology but in a literal sense.'

'And then he made some comments on the landscape you were, so to speak, sharing.'

'Yes. How static it was as if it had been created like that yesterday or a million years ago and seemed so fixed and unalterable. Yet, strangely enough, we geo-morphologists were the ones trying to chart its slow changes, its impermanence. I'm not sure I agree, but it's just the start of a conversation, isn't it? The rockfall put a stop to that.'

'This might be a wrong tack, but can I tell you what my research involves? I think there is some connection.'

'You know, I've never been quite sure what it is you are doing over the last year. Too preoccupied with the Niger expedition.' I am trying to compensate for my selfish distractions.

In fact, all the confiding that Alice and I have done in the past few weeks has been one-sided. I find it easy to confide in her, but then afterwards it is as if some sort of brake has been put on our relationship. A coolness followed. Affection seems a luxury.

Even our sleeping together is hardly a comfort. It is almost as if she would have preferred not to have been confided in. There is little return of confidence on her part too. Or isn't there anything there in her scheme where I might have some insight? Or just comfort.

However, she begins to tell me again about the new work she is doing on the brain. Straight reporting. It isn't medical work in the sense of treating illnesses. More like primary research into how our brains work in relation to the lives we are living and what we perceive around us. No cutting open of people's skulls.

I knew that of course. Her work is all charts and screens and recorded conversations. I suppose that Joanne will be a better listener than I am. She can ask pertinent questions when the sheer vocabulary nearly defeats me.

'I'm really very much at the learning stage,' says Alice. 'I still suspect that she is simplifying things for my sake. Apparently, the human brain along with the brains of most advanced animals has two hemispheres. They are separate in some ways and yet of course interact. But the difference between the two is more marked in humans.

'First, the left side is more concerned with the factual, with analysis, and could almost be described as impersonal, cool, fixed in its concepts, an either/or mechanism. Things are black or white. It is very confident but disengaged emotionally. It stores ideas and rules aided by a concrete vocabulary and grammar. It uses data to work things out logically, even mathematically. It isn't particularly sensitive to changes over time. Especially not to gradual almost imperceptible change.'

'So am I a left-side person?'

'I think that is oversimplifying things. We all use both sides of the brain. But we allow one side sometimes to dominate. Let me explain about the right side.'

'Continue Professor.'

'I'm not lecturing you, Harry? I'm only just getting a handle on all this myself. I can't presume…'

'Go on. What you were saying makes a lot of sense to me. I only used the word Professor as a joke. You sound very convincing. Please go on.'

She goes on to tell me how the right side of the brain operates. It is like a parallel but dissimilar world inside our heads. The generality of information is more important than the detail. Things unfold and change in time. They are organic, alive and very importantly, connected to others.

Consequently, it is less precise, sometimes incomplete, often unresolved. The focus is on the in-betweenness of things. And our thoughts are invaded by hunches, imaginative ideas, poetry if you like. It picks up words from the left side of the brain to create images, metaphors, impressions.

And even as it reasons, it is prepared to give ground, admit more than one answer and look for middle ground. Grey areas. Inconclusiveness, even woolliness, along with the important role of sentiment, the unknown, even the mystical.

'All those intangible things. The ones I probably suppress?'

'No, you don't. That's the point. Why on earth have you been impressed by some strange Tuareg's description of the landscape, if you didn't have a passion for it yourself? I've heard you talk about the places you've visited. It's much more than the rocks and strata.

'And now, when your son comes home in disgrace, you listen to him and don't show him the door. I think you would like to understand him. When Thomas gets involved in some kind of escapade, I bet it is his right side of the brain misbehaving. *He* certainly needs to get the balance right.'

'Well, he is our son.'

'Exactly. But it is always about balance. For all of us.'

'Wonderful food for thought. Cows have two stomachs, we have two brains. Why not?'

'But it can be dangerous to draw conclusions hastily. Our knowledge of the brain is in its infancy.'

'But you still haven't told me what your research now involves.'

'We are looking at how the brain helps us to hear music. How is it that deaf children and autistic ones can respond to music in many ways? Both technically in the manipulation of rhythms and emotionally in the flow and overall character of the music. Not that their responses are one or the other. They work in tandem.'

'And which side of the brain is conducting all this?' I ask. 'Both sides. In fact, when we listen to music and respond to it, our whole brain becomes alive. It's all to do with interaction and cooperation. The scans show this clearly. A dozen places in the brain will be illuminated.

'Even when the person is completely deaf, she can respond to the remembered sounds inside her head. Children deaf from birth seem to have some sort of library of music. Though we don't quite know what stimulates it. It is probably all connected with the tactile. A considerable percentage of the population may be deaf or blind, but people who are tactile-deaf so to speak are very rare. Somehow as long as you are alive your awareness of texture and movement is at work. Your whole body is an organ, a sounding board.'

We all sit there and ponder that. I play a piece with my fingertips on her arm, but she draws her arm away. Then Joanne says, 'You remember how I had piano lessons when I was l little. I didn't stick with it. Something didn't click.

'Well, I've started again. I've only got an electronic keyboard. I can even turn the sound down while I practise. There's a lot of teasing… from some of the others. "Is that Joanne on the Joanna?" But I find it's really the best thing for unwinding.'

81

'What started you on that?' asks Alice.

'Well, there is a music student I've been talking to. From one of the other flats.'

'Ah, I see. Male I presume.'

'That is not the point, but yes. He's Czech.' It is clear from her manner that Joanne does not wish to go into further detail. So I change the subject and pose the question: 'And how does the brain go to sleep?'

'Oh dear,' says Joanne. 'I bet that is even more baffling.'

Alice nods 'Quite another story. Let's do an experiment and try going to sleep and report back in the morning.' And we troop off dutifully. Alice turns immediately to compose herself for sleep. So much for my using her arm as a keyboard.

10

Alice

Harry and I decided to go for a walk in Swaledale. We took the car to Gunnerside and parked up before following the river upstream. We waved to a tractor driver who was ploughing an adjacent field. Two jets overhead were skimming the Moreland edge.

'I thought we came here for the peace and quiet,' said Harry ruefully.

At one point, the valley narrowed, and the trees overhanging made a sort of tunnel. I remember looking at Harry and thinking that he looked apprehensive. Then suddenly the whole of the tunnel exploded into a vortex of sound. We both clapped our hands over our ears and instinctively crouched down, almost falling to our knees. Then the kit was gone, with a weird throbbing after-effect. We both looked at each other. Harry's face was twisted and unseeing.

'Those jets,' I said. 'Flying low up the valley like that. It ought not…' But I didn't finish. Harry sat down abruptly on the ground, speechless. He was still holding his ears.

'Can't hear a thing,' he said.

'Give it time,' I said. 'It'll come back.' He looked at me blankly. Then he got to his feet again and without saying anything more to me began to walk back down the valley. I followed meekly in his footsteps. As we passed the tractor again, grinding along the hillside, Harry gestured towards it.

'Nothing,' he said.

We were just a few yards from the car when suddenly Harry staggered, as if he were drunk, and then sat down on the tarmac. He leant forward and vomited between his knees. Then he shook his head, staggered to his feet and apologised. We managed to get him cleaned up.

I shouted to him, mouthing the words, 'Can you hear me?'

'Only just.'

I drove us home in silence of course. Once we were home, we made a drink and unfroze a meal. Harry seemed to pick up a little, and he could get what I was saying as long as I faced him and made it very simple.

'Doctors tomorrow!' I said, mimicking a stethoscope. He nodded and then pointed to the bedroom. He was asleep by the time I had cleared things up and joined him.

The morning after the walk, Harry got up quite early and was sitting in the kitchen drinking coffee when I came down. He said his head was still full of porridge, and there was buzzing in his ears. I had a notepad and jotted down some basic questions... in preparation for our visit to the doctor. How much could he hear? With which ear? Had he been sick like that again? The vertigo?

Apparently, yes, once in the night. No, he had slept badly and had actually dreamt about Niger, if that were relevant. Nothing specific. I rang the GP and made arrangements. We were in luck, and we were able to drive in for a mid-morning consultation.

The GP looked into his ears. No wax. Something vestibular, he said. Maybe viral. There were some tablets to control the nausea. He couldn't at that point say more. An appointment was made to see the specialist in a week's time. When we got home, I phoned the children to put them in the picture. I didn't mention the vertigo yet.

'Do I need to come home?' Joanne said in alarm. I reassured her that everything was under control. Best to wait to see what the specialist had to say. 'I can manage here, for the time being. The Research Centre can wait. I've spent half my life there, this year and last.'

When I spoke to Thomas, to tell him about his dad's deafness, he seemed quite shocked. As if there were some connection with the trouble, he had brought home. No doubt he was still contemplating his fall from grace, along with the absence of Porsche and fabulous Indian girlfriend. He said that he could stay in the flat till the end of the month. Meanwhile, he was on the lookout for a different career path.

'Not something in the city. Where all the money is. No sir!' he said in a forlorn sort of way. Thomas is always good at acting parts.

'So are you looking into the whole business of retraining?'

'I'm giving it some real thought.'

I gave him a brief account of our walk, the planes, and our subsequent visit to see the specialist. I specifically avoided connections with the Niger trip or with his city dismissal.

'How dreadful,' he said. 'Shall I come down? It's not as if I'm overloaded with work.'

I told him to wait for the specialist's fuller report. A few days later, we were at the hospital. There was a lot of waiting. Harry sat there with a slightly bemused look on his face. There had been a bout of vertigo before we left home it came only once a day.

The ENT specialist was Indian and examined Dad thoroughly, ears, eyes and throat. Then it was blood tests, more eye tests in another department, and a scan was planned for a few days' time. There were lots of questions about Dad's lifestyle, his golf and walking, his diet and his alcohol consumption. The experience in the Pennine Valley with the aircraft was discussed.

Finally, the specialist sat us down for his final diagnosis. Harry stared straight at the doctor and seemed to be following it all by some sort of guesswork. I had my notebook in case we needed it.

As always, it was all very inconclusive. We were to wait for the blood tests and the scan. The most probable diagnosis was going to be Meniere's or some vestibular infection. The vomiting and nausea coupled with the loss of hearing and what Dad had called a "porridgy" feeling ("fullness" was apparently the correct term) pointed that way. But it would be difficult for him to make a final diagnosis.

But, still, everything was pointing to the Meniere's syndrome a term (as understood by the medical profession, not by me), for a group of symptoms with no clear cause. Appropriate accents on the letters "e" but I can never remember quite which. It was a condition of the cochlear in the inner ear. Its battery of membranes was damaged and not working properly. We managed to get this across to Harry with the aid of my notepad and a quick sketch done by the doctor.

'But where has it come from?' he asked, as if it were something alien. Which of course it was.

'Any one of several causes. A virus.' (The doctor wrote these down on the pad.) 'A sudden input of sound, high decibels, like your aeroplanes. Or exposure to continuous sound in your workplace.' (Three more explicit notes).

He consulted his screen. 'I see, you're retired, and in any case. I hardly think geology presents any hazardous situations. Do you play in a Brass band or orchestra? No. Well, the aircraft noise you experienced would be unlikely to be a root cause, but it may have acted as a trigger. Deterioration would already have been underway. Have there been other problems?'

'Well, I have had some tinnitus, and feeling unsteady. As if I were tipsy.'

'That fits in,' the doctor says. 'So we have to look more closely at your heart. Then there may be contributory factors… any recent emotional or work-based upsets?' Harry glanced at me and then said no. I presumed that we were for the time being leaving rockfalls and son-falls from grace out of it.

And then the doctor gave the coup de grace. 'Or,' he said, 'it could be any combination of those causes I've outlined. Or even all of them together.' I thanked him on Harry's behalf, trying to keep the irony from my voice.

'How do you like that?' said Harry when we were back in the car. He had read through my notes. 'Have I got this right? Virus, or big aircraft bang or emotional shock. Or too much heavy metal. All four possibilities. Four answers all of which may be right. Even all of them at the same time! Talk about getting a cut-and-dried answer.' We tried to laugh at what seemed like the idiocy of it but only managed a mirthless groan.

'We didn't tell them anything about the rockfall in Niger,' I wrote on the pad.

'Best not. For the time being. It may not be connected.'

'I don't think it will be,' I said. But I wasn't being truthful. Harry's behaviour since his return from Niger had been so strange, so unsettling. The specialist had mentioned "stress". The idea of something working away and then triggering the hearing failure would have to be taken into account at some point.

But perhaps I was letting my imagination run away with me. I also wondered whether Harry's train of thought and my preoccupation with my joint university scheme might have made a contribution.

Back at home, I prepared a quick meal, but then Harry had one of his bouts of vertigo and had to sit it out in the armchair. I sat next to him, as the chair was quite wide, and I was amazed at how strongly he held onto my hand as if he were holding onto a lifebuoy. We sat there for half an hour, and only then did he let go, with an apologetic mumble. It was after nine before we ate the meal which was almost inedible. He began to thank me for the way for staying close to him.

I managed to smooth that over. We knew how each other felt and always had, there was no need for thanks. I realised how much we operated together by instinct. Even if there was a coolness to our relationship at present. In any case, it had never really worried him that I was often preoccupied with my work.

Some people would call me bossy. But not people who know me, least of all Harry. I sometimes wondered if our periods apart made our relationship more relaxed and accepting than the one we had now where I had to be so attentive and sympathetic.

Harry said that he had to go to bed, he was dog-tired. I stayed up till ten watching, of all things, snooker. Those guys knocking balls. It all seemed so unhurried and logical. Decisions about angles and cue power and safety shots.

Yet I suppose they have their emotional problems. How to deal with all the cash they make. The adulation of the crowd? Perhaps once at that table, they put those behind them. Wired up for pure right brain activity.

11

Alice

The next few months were a trial. The attacks of vertigo were daily and lasted for just over half an hour. Harry learnt to sit tight and do nothing. The tinnitus came in unpredictable episodes and sometimes kept him awake. Several times in the night I woke to find the lights on, and he would be sitting looking at the wall bleakly, or he would be trying to read.

'I can't bloody read with this racket going on,' he said.

'What about a word game?' I said. As if he were a child.

'Alright,' he said. 'What do we start with?'

'Fruits,' I said. 'A is for Apple.'

'B is for bloody banana!' the reply, and I thought at least there is a bit of defiance there. Then we tried the capital cities of countries and the names of famous sportsmen. I had to write most of the ones I came up with. After a while, he said the noise was beginning to subside. Then he began to tell me about the noise.

I listened because he seemed to quite enjoying making a drama of it, in an absurd way. He categorised them according to severity. Like storms. Category One: mild attack… almost tranquilising, like the murmur of storm waves on a distant beach.

Or like a large orchestra playing an unending pianissimo chord, which keeps trying to resolve itself but never can. Category Two: a freight train of empty wagons rattling through a tunnel. Category Three: someone with a Black and Decker trying to get inside your skull. Eventually, he lay down and said he might sleep, and we both must have dozed off eventually.

Although the dizzy spells and tinnitus came and went, the hearing loss was constant and, as we came to realise after some other appointments, unlikely to be reversed. He had given a clever little hearing aid which he seemed to master quite quickly and was given a badge which said "I am deaf", as if he was himself unable to utter the words. At first, he refused to wear it. There was talk of lip-reading classes though difficult to pin someone down about it.

I wasn't keen on leaving the house but Joanne came home once or twice on flying visits. I was able to dash off to appointments back in London. The rest of the time I managed things from my laptop, but it was not very satisfactory. Thomas came home eventually to stay. He described visiting a job centre where a kindly Asian interviewed him. The man folded his hands on the desk as if in prayer and smiled encouragingly.

'I just want any job,' Thomas told him. 'Locally. Just for the present. Mustn't have anything to do with money or banks. In fact, as far away from those sort of places as possible.'

'But you have a degree in law. And your work experience is in the financial world.'

'Okay, but I don't want that to restrict me.'

'But you shouldn't ignore these things. It would be a waste of your talents and training.'

'It's no big deal. I just want a temporary job. For a few months. Of course, I have huge plans in the long term to return to the world of high finance and make a fortune. Probably in Brussels or Switzerland.'

He saw that the man suspected he was not being serious. He shuffled some papers and handed one that was about working in a supermarket. There was a management training scheme.

Thomas showed me the papers. It looked totally unsuitable. But he contacted them and was called for an interview, somewhere in London. At the interview a few days later, he told them he had resigned from the job because he found the city stressful to work in. I bet they looked at him and thought, stressful for whom? He was banking on his previous employer giving him a clean record.

The fraud wouldn't be something they would want to draw attention to. So a supermarket? Not one of the big ones. A supervisory post, whatever that might be? And local. How local? The bit about management training didn't impress either me or Harry. When I told Thomas this he just said, well that's three of us.

'Of course, I'll look for something better,' Thomas said. 'And I'm still looking into the idea of going back to college. Something quite different. But still connected with the law.'

Joanne rang to say that she was coming home for several days again, not just a weekend. It would give me some respite. Harry wasn't helpless, but it seemed wrong to leave him on his own. I was able to make flying visits to Birmingham and Manchester, talking one-to-one with people who were going to be the mainstay of the scheme.

Whenever Joanne came she was always a great comfort to Dad, in a way that Thomas couldn't be. But Joanne herself quite easily gets upset. Talking to her dad was difficult for her. I hadn't realised that I could undertake quite happily a two-way shouted conversation with a lot of gestures with Harry, with the occasional aid of the notepad. But, apparently, Joanne's voice was much quieter and at a different pitch, and Dad could not tune into it. She tried with the notepad, but it was hopeless for long exchanges.

One day, someone came round and took him off for golf. 'You don't need to be able to hear to play golf, do you?'

By now, the vertigo was a bit less frequent. If it hit him out there on the greens all he had to do was to sit down for a while. He came back gloomier than ever. The ribbing and the jokes out in the open for him were non-starters. Some of them had tried to engage him in small talk; later, there was the clubhouse.

He found the chatter on all sides impossible, along with the clink of glasses and rattle of cutlery. There was some kind of Muzak which they did manage to get the person at the bar to turn down. But it was still intrusive. Strange, he could not hear it, and yet it upset him. He had pleaded tiredness and someone brought him home. Another session was mooted but nothing came of it.

At this point, Harry once again picked up on the philosophy book. Once he asked me if I knew the difference between theology and philosophy, and I struggled with that. 'Someone who believes by having faith and insight, without rational deduction, and someone who relies on what he observes and works out in his own head, using deduction?' That was my suggestion, and I wrote it on the pad. 'But,' I added, 'I suspect that theologians and philosophers use both faith and deduction in their deliberations. No such thing as a single-minded approach for either of them.'

I wrote that pennyworth down on the pad. I knew it wasn't a satisfactory answer. He looked at it and then said: 'Perhaps we as human beings have to do both of them at the same time,' which echoed my thoughts. 'Overlap, in-betweenness, uncertainty,' I wrote on the pad. 'Key words. Nothing ever cut and dried.'

He wrote on his pad: 'Some disputes and situations don't resolve themselves. Neither side can see their way to a compromise. There is no satisfactory resolution. You have to accept that.' This was getting into some kind of philosophical discourse. What would people think if they saw our scribbling? But somehow, it gave us a position to work from. Or so we thought.

On another occasion, he asked me what I thought "karma" was.

I wrote down, 'No idea really. Being laidback, cool, not being anxious?'

He shook his head. 'I think it's a bit more than that. I must read that chapter again.' I hoped that he knew where he was heading.

Over the next few weeks, the spells of vertigo became less frequent and his head felt clearer. But the deafness, of course, persisted and became worse. At the hospital, both Meniere's or as the specialist unhelpfully said, a Meniere's-type syndrome, was finally confirmed, with words like vestibular and migraine added on. He had tablets, and he had to watch his salt intake.

To celebrate a period of a few days with less frequent vertigo, a joint visit to the supermarket was planned. It proved quite an experience. I made two lists, one for me and one for him. When I got to the tills he was standing there looking uncomfortable. The supervisor, seeing Dad's Deaf badge, had elected to help him, roaring out instructions to the girl on the till as if she were deaf too.

'Do I look helpless?' he asked once we were back in the car.

'Of course not. Some people just never get the balance right. Either too helpful or not helpful at all,' I said with a flurry of gestures.

He nodded. 'I suppose it's better than people ignoring you completely. Talking over your head as if you were a cabbage or a horse.'

Back at home, he seemed to get some satisfaction working with his sketchbook. He had a whole battery of drawings from Niger. Usually, he only scribbled a few notes at the bottom of his sketches, but now he started to write a descriptive piece, almost like a guide to a traveller who might visit the place.

He explained to me one evening what he was thinking. 'I could put in a lot more background if I researched it. I must read again what Hockney had to say about his deafness and sense of perspective. Oh and on another tack, I once read a monograph on the Arizona Desert.

'A Victorian scientist's travel journal with beautiful sketches. The text itself was a literary masterpiece. There were some photographs too, but they were poor. No sense of distance or proportion. But the nineteenth century, imagine that! Their cameras couldn't deal with great distances.'

'I think the extended sketchbook is a brilliant idea,' I said.

'A what idea?'

'Brilliant. As in a star.' Eventually, he did understand.

There were all his other books of sketches. Even the British ones like Arran, the Pennines and the Welsh border. Then those from abroad in Yugoslavia, as it was then, from Sicily and Corsica.

'Illustrated guidebooks. I suggested. For those who would like a bit of geological meat to chew on,' I suggested. He looked blank. What was the word "chew" doing in that sentence? Then I wrote it down, and he grinned when he had read it…

'But,' he said, 'who would read it?'

'I don't know. You would have to investigate the market.'

'Mark what?'

I wrote the word MARKET on his pad. He looked at it and grunted.

'But, first, you would really want to do it. You know…'

I wrote the words "really want to do it" and then, in capitals ENTHUSIASM on his pad.

'Yes,' he said. 'That's the real problem. Perhaps when all this…' He whirled his hands round his head like a helicopter… 'has subsided.'

On several occasions, I found him asleep on the couch in the study and had to persuade him to come to bed. But then he suddenly put all the sketchbook stuff onto one side and almost seemed to forget about it. But there was one upside; he was determined to face up to the clear and measurable challenge of his deafness. It was something that could be pigeon-holed. Something he could handle. His notorious left side would be good at that.

If his moments of gloom and helplessness were less frequent, there were still bad days. 'Just hold my hand, Alice,' he would say. 'That's what keeps me sane.'

And the calm that came then almost brought me to tears. We were not very emotional people with each other. That was not our way. But I knew that I was in this with Harry now, just being supportive wasn't enough. I had in a way to be deaf too. It brought us closer than we had ever been.

One day, Joanne and I discussed the possibility of trying to get Harry back to the notebooks. Joanne suggested broadening Harry's remit. Why not look at the landscape from an aesthetic viewpoint, through poetry and music too?

'Oh dear. Great idea but let's be cautious about this,' I said. 'At the moment, he seems to have dismissed the whole project. That sort of suggestion might put him off forever.'

But it did set me thinking about what I had once known about the composers who revelled in painting sound pictures. I wish I had taken more notice. Aren't they called tone poems? I googled it and made a list. There was Debussy, Sibelius, Russians like Mussorgsky.

Then there were the modern English composers like Elgar, Britten and Vaughan Williams. I was on a flight of fancy of course; I hadn't listened to that kind of music for years. But this was some of the music that we, especially the music specialists among us on the scheme, were employing in our studies of the brain. I should have been more aware of them and made a point of listening to some of them.

There were links here with therapy… so surely it would be of help to Harry. Then I stopped. What was I thinking? Stupid me; he won't be able to hear them anyhow.

I quickly made a list of poets that I remembered vaguely from my school days: Wordsworth, Dylan Thomas, Houseman, and R.S. Thomas. Then those English composers… it all seemed a bit of a wild fancy: Classical Music and Poetry. They never had been Harry's real cultural interests. But who was I to try to circumscribe or pre-judge? He would find his own way in all this.

When I showed him both lists he seemed quite interested in these new connections. 'But you would have to listen to the music for me and write something up. Perhaps for the poetry too, if I have difficulty in understanding it.'

My memory of the poets was very sketchy. The composer's mere names. In fact, at that point, I had a vision of myself as a real academic charlatan introducing music into our scientific investigations without being familiar with it. Resolved to remedy that.

As for the poets, perhaps Joanne was a better source. Joanne still loved poetry in spite of the move away from literature into medicine. As she often said, the divide between arts and science is a false one anyhow.

There was one occasion, late in the evening, when Harry showed me a particular sketch. It was of the wadi and escarpment in Niger, with the desert receding into the distance. There were several ink crosses mid-landscape.

'That's where we stood with the Tuareg, you know, when we were speaking to them. I don't know whether I could add convincing human figures to the sketch. I was never any good at that. But I can see them, especially the young man, as clear as I can see you. And the things he said are fresh in my head. The annoying thing is that we have no decent photos or sketches before the event. What a missed opportunity!'

Then he pushed the sketch back into his folder, and I knew it wasn't the time to pursue it.

12

Alice

Joanne and I arranged to meet in St Albans and have a chat over coffee. I could then go on to London for a meeting. We met in a cafe in town some distance from her surgery. I told Joanne that Thomas seemed to be settling down quite happily in his supermarket job.

She said that Thomas still thought of his downfall in the city as a game that he lost, a wheeze that backfired. 'I can't even understand what the game is all about, nor how serious the breaking of the rules is,' Joan said with a laugh. 'Whenever he talks about it, he implies that it is something everyone is doing, and he is unlucky to be caught. On the moral aspect of it all... a form of thieving I call it... he just hums and has and makes no reply. However, it is clear that he no longer wants to be involved in finance, or "play the markets" as he calls it. Too risky.'

I tell her that he is looking for something to pursue which would give him a buzz without the illegality. One option is to go back to the law.

'Why law again?' she says, dumbfounded. 'He didn't enjoy that the first time, did he? He'd have to buckle down to all those rules and procedures and goodness knows what.'

'He says he can do it,' I told her. 'He's not stupid. This time he would probably have a clearer idea of where he was heading.'

'Can you picture it? Thomas being methodical following procedures watching every word that he said or wrote?'

'I know. But, at the same time, you know he's now talking about involvement in environmental issues. And civil liberties. Where and what are the limits? How far can they be exploited and how far the activist can work against those people who exploit it illegally?

'That's just the kind of talk that will excite him. How does the law define people's right to protest? How far you can push against the law if you've got some moral right on your side. And then course, he wants to go for the big companies who rip off the environment, protecting themselves with their phoney lawyers. He knows those people he says, he knows how they think. He can't wait to get his teeth into them.'

'Good luck to him,' said Joanne. 'It does sound a bit like the crook who converts to a policeman.'

We talked about the "signing" experts who helped with a profoundly deaf patient of hers. 'Would there be any mileage in getting someone like that for Dad?' she asked. 'Or at least someone to teach him lip-reading? After all, he is actually already beginning to do it, isn't he? In the way, we all do every day of the week, subconsciously. Especially in noisy environments. I'll see what more I can find out. How is Dad, in a general way?'

I explained to her how positive her dad was in relation to his deafness. He had a clear target. The signing would be something for him to get his teeth into. And things were a little better on the geology front. He was getting back to his sketches and notes.

But there's still that lack of real enthusiasm. With that, he needed a specific target. Something down to earth. Strange really to be trying to persuade a geologist to connect with the Earth!

'While you, Mum, are having to struggle to keep up with your three universities scheme.'

'Yes, but we are getting to a point where it may actually take off. I'm going to need to give a lot of attention, and your dad knows that. He's coping really well. We'll be okay, the two of us.'

The surgery, Joanne said, with its long hours gobbled up all her time and energy. Her hours were fragmented and inconvenient, and she still attended lectures at the hospital for training in some technical areas.

Then she mentioned Petr again. 'He's Czech by the way and is studying at the RCM. He plays piano but aspires to be a composer. Lives in an adjacent flat. We met at a party in the same building. It was a noisy affair… not my cup of tea. Amazing that we met at all, as I rarely go to parties and never stay for long. But we just happened to be thrown together, and he said: "You don't look as if you are enjoying yourself."

'We sat outside on the steps of the block of flats and chatted. Silly really, I ended up telling him about Dad and Thomas… within the first few minutes of meeting him. He looks embarrassingly like Kafka, the dark hair, those eyes and cheekbones. But he is a good listener.

'I wonder if all musicians are. He told me a bit about his life in the Czech Republic, his father was a Pastor in a city church. His mother is a teacher of disabled children. He's an only child and has always known that he would pursue a musical career.'

I asked her what sort of music he wrote.

Joanne screwed up her face. 'He uses the word minimal. New to me, in relation to music. It involves strings and percussion, the piano and gongs. Very plain and unadorned, but religious, almost ritualistic.

'He mentions Arvo Pärt, the Estonian composer… as an influence. I have never heard of him. Eventually, another friend and I went to his flat and listened to some of the music. People sing single notes or a phrase over and over again. And the gongs of course which resound for ages in the rich acoustic of some church.

'Then Petr played some of his own pieces. I didn't quite know what to make of them, so very desolate and bleak. I couldn't work out whether there was any real rhythm or momentum. Just long sustained chords, gradually shifting and then thin melodic fragments. But I am getting used to it.

'Eventually, Petr and I make it a regular thing… a kind of music club, and we listen to other less challenging music… Bach, Beethoven and Schubert, but then Messiaen, Stravinsky and Bartok too. Most of it is quite new to me. Not always easy music to listen to. There's one piece he mentioned by Varese called "Desert" with a French pronunciation. Very modern and almost brutal with great sliding slabs of sound. Do you think Dad would listen to it?'

I said that he might. 'But come on now,' I said, 'I want to know about your piano playing.'

'Well, I didn't get far with it the first time, did I. But with Petr I seem to be making progress.'

'That's good.'

'And I have begun to take an interest in poetry too. Petr is very keen.'

She said she had read out one poem to him, by the poet Edwin Muir who died in 1959. It is about our seeking out a sense of time, of life and death.

But pilgrim man
Travels foreknowing to his stopping place
Awareness on his lips, which have tasted sorrow,
Petr planned to set it to music.

There was another poem by Muir, she said, a famous one, called "Horses", written in the 50s about a post-Nuclear Age. She wondered if Dad would read that. It was so full of hope, renewed life… in the midst of an imaginary scene of utter desolation. The Poet was Scottish but lived in both Dresden and Prague for a time, and he and his wife were responsible for the translation of German novels, especially those by Kafka.

'By the way,' she said, with a giggle, 'that business of me seeing a resemblance to Kafka in Petr, you must keep that to yourselves. Petr isn't in the least a haunted figure like a novelist. But his seriousness and that intent look always remind me of him. You know I can talk about Dad's experience and all that and Petr seems to understand. He says that he will be looking into Muir and the Czech connection. He says that the study of poetry, and certainly music, is a good training for anyone wanting to become a doctor or a teacher. You learn to listen and look into someone else's mind and emotions… things that may be hidden.'

She said that the piano was still something of a battle, but she was making progress, and she and Petr managed some duets and arrangements of Bach and Schubert. But the tricky fingering kept her awake at night! She even suspected her fingers were twitching away when she was examining patients. 'What will the poor souls think?' she said with a grin.

Hearing the way Joanne talked of Petr made me realise that it was something quite serious for her, even though the notion of being in love seemed a kind of luxury which she said she couldn't afford. But perhaps things will improve with time. After they have played the duets in his flat, they share a takeaway meal. If she is not on an early shift, she stays overnight.

In other words, they are pretty much bound up with each other. They have talked about the luxury of a holiday. Petr couldn't afford the money, she couldn't afford the time. But they would work something out. Perhaps France or Italy.

On the cheap. Petr said they might even go back to his home and meet his parents. I think she was not quite ready for that. But he would love to meet us two, and I said, absolutely, any time. It was a comfort for me in a way, to see young love flourishing.

13

Harry

I suppose you could say I am getting acclimatised to the Meniere's or whatever it is. The spells of vertigo now come only every other day or so, and I can recognise the signs of their onset, and take evasive action. During the spells, there is nothing that I can do except sit tight. The vomiting is much less frequent now. But the deafness persists, and it seems to be getting worse. I am provided with a more powerful hearing aid which amplifies the sound but proves very noisy, sometimes distracting, and always tiring.

There is one shaft of light, although a modest one. After a fruitless visit to London in order to talk to some people, he knew Thomas shows us a letter from the University of Edinburgh. He has been offered a place to study for an MA in the specialist area of environmental law. I have never thought of Thomas as having green credentials, or even an awareness of such issues. But he tells me he has been reading on the subject.

'I tend to have worked with the sort of people who probably see the environment as some kind of sack of Christmas presents; first come, first grab and grab again. As if it will always be replenished. They can afford the best lawyers, the ones who know how to cheat the system,' he said. 'I think I know how they think and manoeuvre. I'm ready to give them some aggro.'

I hear most of this loud and clear. Thomas is always very audible. So the one who has cheated the system is now out to catch the others who cheat but on a more massive scale. I'm not sure whether it is a change of heart or mere opportunism, but I am prepared to give him the benefit of the doubt. We talk about money. Apparently, he has savings and the money from his Porsche, but a modest contribution from me is going to help.

'I'll pay you back of course.'

'I don't suppose these environmental people will pay big money?'

'We'll have to see won't we?'

'By the way, you'll need some wheels,' I say.

'Sorted. Garage near the supermarket today.' Fair enough.

'What sort of thing?'

'Wait and see.'

That evening we go outside to inspect. There stands a yellow and white VW van, somewhat the worse for wear. 'Good for protests!' he said, caressing its flanks like a Derby winner. 'Nice scratches.' There are some patches of paintwork that were ripe for graffiti.

Back in the house, he tells me via my notepad that he has joined an environmental pressure group. E-watch. They are big on mining. Opencast working in Bolivia, Central Africa; Lithium and Uranium. Destruction of good agricultural land.

Local communities are torn apart. He draws some diagrams showing a new process of in situ recovery, with liquids injected into the ground, and the mineral solutions pumped out. I'd heard about it, but that's all. Thomas seems to think I should know all about it.

Toxins end up in the aquifers. Radioactive sheep and goats. Local people were baffled. Forced to move to new territory where they face other problems.

'So where do your E-watch come in?'

'Watch, miners, limits, greedy,' are the four words I hear, but they are enough. 'Sit-ins, obstruction, newspapers.' Fine, those words make sense too. So is this the way that Thomas and I are going to talk from now on? I think he quite enjoys it. I find it adequate but a bit depressing.

'Not too extreme I hope, I say. Some of these protests go too far.'

'When is trespass a reasonable valid protest?' He writes that down for me. With his lawyer's hat on. I think I see what he's getting at. Sometimes in order to get noticed you have to test the rules out. Laws are boundaries after all; they can be adjusted. 'Environmental protesters need good lawyers,' he says and beams with some pride. Well, I hope he gets there.

Surprising what I can pick up from the pad or by inference. It seems to me that they are indeed going to need good lawyers to face up to the big mining interests, so that is an incentive for Thomas to become a good one. 'Watch out for the lies. Explosives, Pollution, Water Table. Consultation, Bribes. Greed.'

I write these nice angry capitals on the pad and Thomas relishes them. And what do I know? Fatherly interference never got me very far with Thomas. I'm going to have to rely on his good sense. Thomas saves the world by persuasion.

He says he knows the mindset of these guys. Their second cousins worked alongside him in the city. 'Cunning yes; stupid sometimes.' He rubs his hands together in anticipation.

'Interestingly enough,' I say. 'At one time, I thought there might be evidence of all this in Niger.'

'How's that?'

'~~There~~ They thought that an outfit called BZO might be there, undercover,' I tell him.

Thomas gets on his phone for a few minutes. Then he comes back.

'Nah. BZO folded, last year. Hot Water in Bolivia. No interest in Africa.'

In fact, I presume that we will never learn anything about those three vehicles in the desert. Declan is right. The rockfall was just that, as inevitable as anything other phenomenon we study in the desert. In fact, confirmation of all this comes later in with a message from Steffi.

The group of vehicles with their unfriendly drivers we saw in the desert were indeed, rogues. Rogue Scandinavian palaeontologists, miles away from the Chad border where they should have been. No wonder they didn't want to talk. But highly unlikely to be blowing things up.

This really puts an end to my fantasies about BZO. Even that strange sketchy fault line I have reported to Declan seems to be insubstantial. Dismissed.

To get back to Thomas' plans, I am pleased with them. They seem to have a purpose to them. I know that he likes a fight, but he will presumably be on the right side of it. More or less. Where has he got that from? More probably from his mother.

After all, the rocks and landscapes I deal with never answer back, never rebel. Except of course, on a geological timescale when there is flooding, earthquakes, volcanic eruptions and continental shift. And rockfalls to flatten a Tuareg encampment. But, actually, there is much more in the news now. All this talk of unstable weather patterns, of drought and desiccation and sea-level rises through climate change and what Governments ought to do about it.

And then, perhaps the most worrying because out of our control, is the role of the multinationals. Perhaps people like Thomas should come into their own. See justice is served. I'm still not quite sure whether he is quite the best person here.

Or am I being unkind and negative? Surely he needs our encouragement. Later on, I talk about this with Alice when she is not busy on her laptop. She has the same reservations about David's new enthusiasm. But she agrees with me, he needs our support.

'Support? Encouragement? I wonder. Does a Centurion tank need to be coaxed?'

But after another week it is confirmed that Thomas's place at Edinburgh is due to start in January. Alice and I congratulate him. Even if we both metaphorically have our fingers crossed.

14

Harry

Thomas has moved up to Edinburgh, ahead of the course. He rings us at the weekends, and Alice talks to him. Or rather he talks to her. He is involved with a new protest group, GEOGUS. A play on the word gorgeous.

We don't ask how relevant that is. And what about E-watch? Useless people apparently. All talk. No, this is a new one. Monitoring mining in South America and Central Africa.

'Tell Dad,' he says to Alice, 'I've been reading up on my geology. Must talk to him about it when I'm next home. Brazil, Peru, Bolivia. Uranium, lithium, that sort of stuff. Brilliant! All this lovely stuff from deep in the earth is injected into the Andes. Why didn't he tell me about it?'

I want to tell him that we never call those minerals "stuff". It amuses me to see Thomas so full of enthusiasm for this new departure. Later, he tells us he is off to Bolivia next month, so he can get back for Christmas and the start of the term in January. A fact-finding mission. Two weeks. In fact, the university are quite keen that he should go, writes Alice on my pad. She takes a deep breath as if summoning up a sober tone of voice.

'There's another factor. A distraction,' she writes on my pad.

For once, I'm not slow. 'What's her name?' She explodes into laughter.

'Agony,' she says. (Well, that is the word that I hear.)

Then she writes it down: 'Antigone.'

'Is she Greek?' I ask.

'I hope she's not so rich that he can't bring her here on a visit?' says Alice finally.

Antigone, I learn from Alice by gradual accretion, is a fellow disciple in Geogus though she is herself studying art. When Alice puts forward the idea of Thomas and Antigone visiting us before South America, Thomas explains that Antigone is quite a wild child in her parents' eyes. Wealthy Scottish family, something in publishing and property. A huge castle somewhere in the middle of the Highlands. If we see her we might be surprised because though she has a generous allowance, she wears the shabbiest clothes, her hair is just a haystack of curls, and she is always adopting down-and-outs in the street, feeding and clothing them.

In the end, she looks like a sartorial disgrace next to them. Her parents despair of her, and she in her way despairs of them. But they still get on alright. And then there's this other thing, Thomas says, and he has forgotten to tell us that she is beautiful. And this is going to be the real thing. The words "beautiful" and "real thing" are left with us to digest.

Alice is still giggling at the last thing Thomas said. She writes it all down for a full effect:

'You know, Mum, I seem to attract rich girls, like bears to honey.' That makes both Alice and I laugh out loud too. I'm glad because I often miss out on jokes. Especially the sort that cease to be funny when you explain them. But the conceit of Thomas. Where does he get that from?

But, overall, the way he talks about Edinburgh is more reasonable, says Alice, as if he is working something out. Let's hope this South American jaunt doesn't distract him. He says his reading for the course is going well. I hope he is being truthful on that score too.

Joanne rings to tell Alice she has made contact with a deaf family who run two-week courses in the North York's Moors. More details later.

'I could get two weeks off in the summer,' writes Alice on the pad. 'We could both go.'

'I don't need someone to look after me do I?'

'That's not the point.' She writes at more length. 'If you are going to sign, I need to learn too. You know, as I told you before conversation. What husbands and wives do?'

'Are you sure that you can afford the time?' I say.

'Yes. Unless of course, you'd rather I didn't,' she says staring at me as if in a challenge.

'I didn't mean that.' One of those many occasions when I don't get it right.

'I have to be honest with you,' she writes finally, 'I'm intrigued.' So when the details come through, we book ourselves up for two weeks in the spring. Apparently, it's a sort of community activity. All the family are involved; George and Cassandra and their two children. Part of the learning is done on the hoof.

Walking talking and signing on the Moors or on the North Yorkshire coast. Or around the house. It sounds a bit weird, like some sort of cult. Suddenly I realise how pleased I am that Alice is going too. Together we can weather a bit of weirdness.

Two weeks later, out of the blue, we get a letter from the British Embassy saying that their representative a Mr Cooper, would like to call on us. Will arrive by car at eleven the next day. Is this going to be something connected with the Tuareg, something Steffi has set up? But then why the British Embassy?

Alas, we discover it is not as simple as that. Four protesting students, Thomas being one of them, have been arrested for trespass and damage to a mining company's property in Bolivia. They were presumably protesting the impact on a local rural community and on the environment of the mining company's activities. The four will most probably be deported. The Foreign Office will keep us informed.

There is nothing in the papers that day, but the next day there is a real splash. GEOKIDS IN BOLIVIAN MINE PROTEST. Kids? It is followed by an official report which suggests that it is all a bit of a jamboree. However, a long article by a science correspondent praises the four protesters for their courage and persistence. The company have a bad name anyhow.

Their work on-site needed much more investigation. Elsewhere a spokesperson for the company says that the well-being of the local communities and protection of eco-systems were their priorities.

'As they would. The name of the company is given: FYG South America. There is a picture of the four of them, David, looking quite heroic, being hustled into a police van, and a wild-looking girl, snatching a protest banner from one of the policemen and waving it aloft, shouting BOLIVIAN PEOPLE

BEFORE GREEDY CAPITALISTS. She is dressed more outrageously than the other three, and she has a mass of unruly red curls. The caption says that her name is "Tig Forsyth". The others, including Thomas, aren't named.'

'Tig? What does that mean?'

'It's what they call her,' writes Alice. 'I can't decide which is more ridiculous Tig or Antigone?'

'And what do they call him?'

'Do you really want to know? Thomas did tell me.'

'I'm going to have to know if it all comes out in the press.'

'The Bull.'

'Oh dear.'

'Hence a sub-headline here, "This Bull's Not for Turning".'

I try to decide, if this strange feeling inside me is disgust or pride.

15

Harry

The lane leading to Clough Farm runs alongside a narrow valley choked with blackthorn, stunted oaks and hawthorn. As the lane peters out and the valley steepens, we are brought in front of the farmhouse. A man in Wellington stands in front of the door, shading his eyes because of the sun. As we clamber out, he reaches out a big hand to us and says. 'I'm George.'

We introduce ourselves. We take out luggage from the boot and follow him into the house. He takes us immediately upstairs to our room which is just a bedroom with barely any other furniture. There is a view up onto the moors from the window. 'Tea downstairs,' he says and then leaves us to unpack. Alice inspects the bathroom which is next door.

Downstairs we clutch our mugs of tea, each emblazoned with a painting of a bird; a kestrel, a blackbird and a plover. George points towards the large wooden table in the centre of the room. 'This where we do it all,' he says. 'Either that or outside,' with a flourish to the window. 'Cass and the kids, back from school, an hour.'

We sip at our tea and make polite appreciative noises about the farm and its location. George speaks with great concentration but in telegram phrases, as if he is rehearsing something, and there is the trace of a Tyneside accent.

'All finished? Rooms.' We troop around the house and find the name of each's function. There are a lot of gestures to indicate washing, sleeping eating. Then the word: "Orientation" comes up, enunciated with much aplomb by George. We follow him outside while he points out the buildings, a farmhouse, a shed, a garage with a small tractor in it and an abandoned caravan that is now a home for the hens.

And the signing begins. There are stone walls, fences, hedges and a small spinney. He accompanies each name with a hand sign. We go back into the house and the wooden table.

'Now on, we sign everything. Pad for writing words down. Okay?' (And he puts up his thumb, and we are invited to imitate.) 'We two both deaf,' he says, 'though I hear some things. Cass nothing, nor the children. But good lip readers. Not me. Cass teacher at many schools. And signs at the university. Durham,' He nods to himself as if is almost incredible. Difficult for us to respond to this, so we just smile and nod too.

George looks us over, almost as if weighing up livestock. Then he seems to relent.

'In an emergency, you talk. Shout. Okay?' More thumbs-up or is it thumb ups? 'And in your room, talk okay.'

There is the sound of a vehicle outside, and we look at the yard from the window as a pickup parks behind our car, and two children leap out with a collie. Young teenagers, shirts flapping, and school hats on backwards. The collie goes to George and then after a pat, finds a niche by the door and curls up. The two children who have rushed into the house come to a halt when they see us. George points at them, and they each come forward with their names, Darren and Chloe.

Then they rush off noisily outside again, tasks being allotted to them by George with a flurry of gestures and occasional words. Then he shakes his head and points his fingers to his mouth, to show how much they talk. He touches his forehead and shakes his head sorrowfully. We understand and nod in agreement. Then Cass comes in.

Can this be the mother of those children? She looks only eighteen years of age, dark hair, sharp-eyed, quick in her movements as if to make up for George's lumbering. She speaks her name, but silently, lips and mouth in perfect enunciation. 'Welcome to Clough Farm. Tea, well, it's dinner really,' she says with a laugh, 'will be in about an hour. Will a lamb stew be okay?'

We respond with the thumbs-up and then she turns to George. The signing flickers between them at breakneck speed and then she goes off to the kitchen. George next. 'Me, jobs to do, You just relax, look round,' and he clumps off outside again. We follow at a distance so as not to get in the way.

But he points out and signs for the hens and the ducks, a dozen sheep in a walled meadow and a vegetable garden with leaks and peppers and potatoes, flanked by soft fruit bushes and a line of apple and plum trees. Then George is busy inspecting and weeding, so Harry and I climb up a bank and get an overall view of what must be Cass and George's small holding. The dog follows us without fuss. As if that is his assignment.

'Can they make a living out of this?' Alice whispers.

'Not much of one. But then Cass is teaching, part-time. And perhaps there are students or paying guests like us.'

'But the brochure said that these courses were a new venture. I wonder what the sign for guinea pigs is if that is what we are?' Suddenly she has the urge to giggle. 'Funny setup, don't you think? Like some cult, no menace, no threats, just silence and flickering palms! They can't be very well off, but there's no hint of poverty. Nor of dissatisfaction or pressure.'

'Anyhow, we're in it for five days. Let's enjoy it.'

We exchange thumbs-up.

The meal is an excellent one. We are offered wine or beer, and we opt for the latter. It comes in a stubby bottle with a sheep's head on it. Darren and Chloe seem to be involved in a signed dispute at the table, all crude pointing and twisting of the fingers, which amuses George hugely, but Cass calls them to order. There is apple and plum pie for pudding.

George gets to his feet and points to the table and mouths the word: "Clear". The children leap to their feet and take everything away, except Cass's place. All done with plenty of clatter and some rivalry. George gestures rather dramatically to the empty table and Cass. She looks both amused and embarrassed, as if she has been announced as a circus act rather than a signing lesson.

But then we get underway. Cass's utensils and plates are the first, as well as the table, chairs, salt and pepper. Then she ranges around the room, curtains, sofa, bookshelves, plants in pots, television (which is hidden under a blanket), door, ceiling, and floor. By now, I am on overload and even Alice looks owlish. But we are saved. Back at the table, Cass reaches for cards from the sideboard, and there we have all the domestic stuff, words with signs, that we need.

Later on, we go into the kitchen where the washing up has been done, and the saucepans kettle cooker frig and washing machine get the treatment. Cass opens the larder, points to the packets and trays and cans of food and says, 'Tomorrow.' I think she means for signing and then not eating. Well, not all of it. Last of all she gives us a card on which the individual signs for each letter of the alphabet are shown, and on the reverse, times and numbers.

When, later that evening, quite early, we retire to our room, I am quite exhausted. Although we have been given permission to talk, we find ourselves talking in whispers and finding it difficult not to laugh.

'Weird,' I say.

'No,' says Alice, 'just… different. Let's look at those cards,' and we test each other out on the letters. I can't work out which way round I should hold my hand when the fingers are showing the numbers. Ten fingers to count from one to twenty? We will need some help with that. We both go off to sleep quickly but then when I awake at six, Alice is already peering out of the window at the moorland edge.

'Come back to bed,' I say. 'You know I feel quite light-headed.'

'Or empty-headed?' says Alice.

I throw a pillow at her and then tug at her slip. Suddenly we are enveloped in each other, aware of the other's bodies, breathless, discarding all clothing, tantalised, then overwhelmed. Afterwards, we lie panting side by side, allowing fingers to trace limbs and faces and breasts. Suddenly there is a rap on the door, and we hear George's shout: 'Tea up.' I put on a dressing gown open the door and find two bird mugs and some biscuits on a plate.

'I'm starving,' Alice says, and we sit up in bed to drink and eat.

'I hope they didn't hear us,' I say, but the absurdity of the observation makes us laugh. How much noise we make would be of no concern to this family.

'I bet that's why you lured me onto this course,' Alice says.

'That's an awful thing to say.'

'I meant it to be,' she says. She pokes me in the ribs.

'Watch out. You'll spill the tea,' I say. 'What's got into you?'

'Nothing. It's this family. They might have a communication problem, it could have been a struggle. But they solve it by sheer exuberance. They love the whole thing… the signing, the rural life, the managing. You can see how George adores Cass.

'And she seems to be able to communicate with him almost without signing. So let it all happen, as they say, and we'll have fun into the bargain. Do you think some of this is rubbing off on us? You and me. Admit it. Things haven't been right with us for weeks now. And suddenly, look at us. Look at you an hour ago.'

'Come on, you too. You were all over me. But seriously. I think I have been a bit envious of you busy with your university scheme, such a serious sense of purpose and organisation. While me, just mooning about doing nothing except replaying my desert nightmare.'

'It works two ways,' she says. 'Perhaps I have been envious too of the grand scale of your problem. Earth-shaking

121

events, skirmishes with fundamental questions of life and death. Wow! By comparison all my concerns, are mere charts and documents and bureaucracy.'

We sup at our tea and eat another biscuit each.

After breakfast, Cass takes the children to school and George proposes to take us on a longer walk. Alice has have forgotten to bring her hiking boots so George finds her a pair of wellingtons which are a bit floppy but manageable. Then we climb the hillside and walk along a ridge to a loose jumble of rocks. George points out the town and a nearby Abbey to the west and the bank of cumulus clouds in the east which he says would be the coast. We sign the words for Town, Church, Sea, moorland, the broad plain (which know-all Harry says, without signing, was an ancient post-glacial lake, a useless fact confirmed however by George), stone, bracken, clouds, wind, and rain (although today is dry).

We see more sheep of course but also birds. Two hovering kestrels which even I can recognise and then a large bird peering at us from the heather in the middle distance. It is a plover. But the same sign seems to do for all birds which is a bit disappointing. Then George finger spells the two birds. There are crows too, and what Harry says are tiny goldcrests bouncing over the moorland, their red patches like sparks in the rough grass. He manages to fingerspell the bird's name.

We return to the bluff overlooking the farm. I try manfully to sign to George; 'Can you make a living here?' and the question sounds crude and intrusive. He waves his hands as if to envelop the whole area of the farm. Is it enough?

But George understands immediately. 'With two children, a struggle.' He wrestles with it. 'But Cass three days, teaching, and special jobs at university. Manage.'

Yet his face is still quite grim, much like the rock-face behind him. 'My wife died four years ago. We have a corner shop near Darlington. She hears perfectly. Then…' and he shrugs. 'No good to stay there. Now, Cass has come to help. We marry soon. Cass likes it here. Me too. And you?'

'It's absolutely splendid,' I say forgetting all about signs. Then we both lay flat hands on our chests as we have been taught and say yes we like it, a lot.

'Good,' says George. And he points back at the farm. 'Next lesson.'

That afternoon, Cass is not teaching, and she gives us a card showing some of the outdoor words we have picked up on our walk. Then we move on to a more taxing vocabulary of verbs; see, walk, like, love, apologise, understand, believe and remember. I am amazed at how much common sense there is in distinguishing between the last three words which involve pointing to the forehead in a particular way.

And then we are on to how to ask a question: Who? What? Where? By the time, we finish out heads are spinning. In spite of the logic of the signing, there is always one signing that seems to be one signed word that defies the logic. The evening is given over to revision, but I seem to have forgotten most of it. I have never been a linguist. Alice is much more proficient. She even seems to be sharing jokes with Cass. And yet I'm the one who is deaf!

Once again we both drop off to sleep quickly. But, then at 6:00, there is bright sunshine striking across the covers. Alice nuzzles up to me amorously. And why not?

The next day, with both Cass and George, we have a morning session on family relationships, and we show them pictures of us as a family, then our grown-up children. Joanne as a doctor and a GP. Thomas as a lawyer. Tricky. Apparently, the sign for a judge involves hands clenched on each side of the head pulling a wig down over our ears.

I try to explain that Thomas is only a little judge which really makes no sense, but then Cass asks what kind of law? I point out of the window with an inclusive and rather flamboyant gesture and then give them the word, Environment. Cass is on to it immediately with a circling hand in front of her body. I say nothing about Thomas's escapade in the city nor about his notorious shenanigans in South America for that matter. Then it is our professions me the geologist (two fists bumped on each other for a G,-*+ and then the hands shaping a globe then shaping the rocks themselves).

Then Alice with the study of the brain. They want to know all about that. It is a struggle but Cass allows her a notepad. She does her big diagram of the brain with the usual labels. They ask her, especially about the ear and hearing. Cass asks about memory. They are very attentive lip readers and readers of our crude signs. Even the children.

Then it was a quite boring session about saying what time it is, then today, yesterday, last week, next year. All fairly confusing. But there is almost always a card for us to take away.

The final full day is supposed to be a trip to the sea but the forecasts are so negative that George takes us to the town. We deliver some leaks and onions to a community stall. There is a bit of signing for the names of fruit and vegetables on the stalls. A look at the old church with a carved doorway.

Alice buys some pastries and chocolate slices. She sends me to the supermarket to buy some wine. I get a reasonable bottle of Puglia red. All this, I am told, is for a party in the evening, to round off our visit.

16

Alice

The last session of the course was a general and light-hearted review of foods, vegetables, cereals, meats and fish. The table was covered with tins and packets as well as the raw materials. Harry said that his mouth was watering as a result. There was an hour before the evening meal which was to be a prelude to the party. George got out a large rather tatty folder and showed his collection of bird pictures.

A few were his own photographs but most were cuttings from magazines and an old calendar. There was a panel against each picture where a numbered diagram showed the sign for each bird. He said he was working on a complete collection and the signs were all his own inventions. Nearly all were imitations of the bird's flight or the manner in which they cocked their heads.

George took us through a few of them. Birds like the kestrel were easy as it hovered, or the long tail of the Yellow Wagtail, the bouncing flight of the goldfinches. For the robin, he pushed out his chest cheekily, like some pompous alderman and for the blackbird imitated rabble-rousing chatter with his fingers.

Elsewhere there were sea birds. I was fascinated by the sign for avocet with George's fingers sweeping from side to side like scoops. 'What about Gannet?' asked Harry and performed a nose-diver into the sea with his pointed fingers.

'Bingo!' said George.

'I've watched them off the north coast of Arran,' said Harry. 'Wonderful rocks. Gabbros, granites, and lava intrusions. And swarms of sea birds.'

George jots down the names of the rocks.

'Love to go back there. But far though,' said George and Harry nodded.

'Yes, it's a bit inaccessible.' (Pause here while the word is found.) 'I love Scotland,' Harry said, and George imitated the bagpipes! Which made us all laugh. 'Actually, Arran is south of Glasgow. I'll show you on the map,' he said casting round for one.

A motoring Atlas was found and the two of them bent their heads to it while Harry listed all the places that were well worth visiting. I helped Cass lay out the food. I found helping out next to Cass both exhilarating and yet calming. Yet you had to be on your toes. And observant.

There were barbecued meats and sausages and vegetables as well as a whole range of pickles and spicy dressings and an assortment of crisps and other nibbles. To follow, a range of desserts from fruit to pastries and ice cream. In the interval, George got out an accordion, and we sang songs like Blaydon Races and Old Macdonald. The second one was of course a real riot with the children and George cavorting in animal antics around the room. Chloe sang a wordless pop song which had a folksy sound to it.

Then George was back with two folk songs, O Waly, Waly (he had to write that one down) and another sad one I had not heard before: 'She's like the swallow.' We didn't know the words, but it was okay to sing la-lah along with them. Cass did not sing at all though she did move to the rhythm of the music and seemed to enjoy it, and she watched George on the accordion as if she were hearing the notes in his fingers or the action of the bellows.

There was Harry's bottle of wine and another one in an unmarked bottle as well as Pepsi for the children.

After our desserts, George announced the entertainment section. He and Cass sat curled up together on an old sofa. Each of us was to tell a story in signs. George disengaged himself from Cass and started things off with a ponderous story about three tortoises in a cafe. It was something to do with the lack of money and the slowness of the creatures.

The children groaned at it... they had heard it before. After applause, Darren was next with an SF Fantasy which was so opaque and full of weird hand and jaw movements that even Cass shook her head in despair. But we all clapped enthusiastically.

Then there was a story from Chloe about a horse that wanted to be a unicorn but never managed more than a bit of a stump on his forehead. But he formed a horse band which was a pop sensation. She rushed to her room and came back with a boldly coloured sketch of the horses in suitably inappropriate pop musician's gear.

It was Cass's turn. 'You must recite,' I said. 'Or show us some of your poetry.'

Cass shook her head and looked at George. 'They are only in sign,' said George. 'Not written down yet.' Another feverish exchange of signs. George was trying to persuade her. And was successful.

What followed took our breaths away. It was swift and elegant but indecipherable. But the expression on Cass's face told us of the grief and the despair that followed a parting, and then some kind of restoration. None of the narrative element was open to us, but all the emotional heft of it was clearly visible in her expressive face and the delicacy of her hand and finger movements. When she had finished, George shook his head and said, 'Wonderful woman!'

Then it was my turn. I asked the sign for "True"… one hand chopping down on the open palm of the other… and then signed and mouthed my way through a family holiday we had enjoyed in Norway. We had stayed on a farm, there were cows to be milked, hedgerows fruits to collect, fish to be purchased from the nearby fjord village, and mountains to be climbed. Cunningly, or so I thought, I was managing to sign my story because it was full of the everyday countryside objects we had learnt the signs for or actions that spoke for words.

And right place for that story? I shrugged, and he took that for yes. Then he launched into it.

He started with "True" and got a laugh. His sawing version was more like "bread" apparently. But then he was into the flights, desert, canyon (which George understood), the heat, the travelling, and then the drilling into the sands. Throughout George was always at hand, picking up on the odd word that Harry scribbled down on the pad. Now came the Tuareg, spelt out letter by letter, the nomads with their black tents and blue gowns and veils, and daggers, and their camels (you've guessed… a couple of wavy humps got a thumbs-up from George).

And the difficult part explaining the conversation Harry had had with the young Tuareg and their mutual appreciation of the unique landscape. How it led to questions about creativity and how the landscapes we admired were merely a moment in a long-running drama. But then he moved abruptly on to the storm and the dreadful collapse of the canyon wall. The entombment of the Tuareg with no chance of recovery. A true story with an unsatisfactory ending. All that discussion and reflection were left in limbo (George got that word straight away and allowed one finger to flick across the other in front of his body).

All the rest of the story Harry told in a sort of Punch and Judy language with his hands. We were all quiet when Harry finished. For the first time, even though I had heard the story several times from Harry, I felt the emotional impact of that utter severance and how it had hit Harry. Cass seemed to be moved too as if she had understood the whole account and also Harry's dilemma in spite of the crudeness of his signing.

Eventually, she signed to George, and he asked. 'Did the whole thing make you unhappy?' (Handheld to the lips and moving down to the chin).

Harry nodded.

'Did they all die?'

'As far as we know.'

'Do you know their names?'

'One was Umar. He was educated…' Harry spelt it out with his fingers. 'Later, we met his parents. But there was nothing that could be done.' I was grateful that Harry didn't go on to talk about the upset of meeting Umar's family and their apparent indifference.

There was another longer pause. Then George signed. 'Coffee? Tea?' But Cass held up her hand. One more question, which she wrote down on the pad.

'Do you love the desert?'

'I think so,' said Harry embarrassed.

Again on the paper, 'And all the others. The mountains, the rivers, the cliffs and the beaches?'

'I suppose so,' said Harry, even more ill at ease.

'Then you must continue that conversation with the landscape and with the Tuareg,' she wrote on the pad.

'But how… I shall never see him again.'

'Continue it through the landscape. Wherever you go. It will be as if he were still there, won't it?'

'Okay,' said Harry. The baffled look on his face might have made me laugh at any other time. But the seriousness of it stifled all humour.

Then there was coffee and a few more songs before we all went off to bed. My sleep was a disturbed one… I couldn't switch off my brain, and my fingers were twitching in concert with each other. Harry however slept like a log.

17

Harry

The next day, we are due to leave the farm at lunchtime. The final revision course lasts for an hour or so after breakfast. The various vocabulary cards we have are checked, and there are a couple of new ones on travel and the colours. Cass is just beginning to explain when there is the sound of a van in the yard.

George goes over to the window. 'Young man and girl,' he says, baffled. When I get up to look, there is the yellow van, Thomas and the girl who I presume is Tig. A mop of unruly hair, almost an Afro, torn jeans, military-style boots.

Alice and I go out to meet them, followed by George. After a brief explanation, they are invited inside. More introductions. Most of my signing evaporates in a flurry of wild gestures, but George and Cass don't seem to mind and welcome the two newcomers warmly. Eggs, toast and coffee appear within minutes, even though they protest.

Over the meal, we try to explain how signing is at the centre of all activity at the farm. Tig is immediately apologetic for upsetting the routine, her sharp features animated under the mop of hair. Her accent is a strange hybrid of upper-class Scots and student slang.

We explain that we are due to leave after lunch; another couple are expected late in the afternoon But we have to complete our final revision session.

'So we must go,' says Thomas. 'Rude to drop in like this. We're talking to a reporter tomorrow, in Edinburgh, from a magazine. You know, about South America. So we really ought to go.'

'Ah,' says Tig, 'but would you mind if we stayed for half an hour and watched your revision,' as if it were some rare treat. Thomas looks aghast at her cheek. 'We wouldn't speak,' she goes on. 'Not a word. Just to see. It's not often you get to see what real signing is.'

George and Cass agree to give that with a hearty thumbs-up before we sit around the table for the final session. The two of them sit silently in the easy chairs and watch. It's hard work for an hour or more, and I am still pretty poor at it, while Alice seems to have remembered so much. In the end, we are told about a conference in Durham which we could attend later in the year. It catered for beginners and the experienced.

Then Thomas and Chloe are on their feet and eager to get away. Alice reminds Thomas that he should come home for a few days, with Tig of course. Then Tig gives Cass and George fierce hugs, and then Alice and I are enveloped and crushed. Even Thomas manages a man-hug for me. Then they are into that custard-hued builders van, and away. We can see Tig steering with one hand, and practising some signs for Thomas's benefit with the other.

An hour later, we too are ready to go on our way. I almost feel tearful, the whole experience has been salutary, and more than that, hugely reassuring in a way that I can't specify. I know Alice feels the same way. Perhaps we have passed some kind of test, and not only in the signing? It is as if we have reached a new sort of understanding. One without demands but with positive expectations; one where we, well especially me, are beginning to learn to sit back and go with the flow.

We trail into the kitchen, and I notice that Alice is absentmindedly touching familiar objects, like the cooker, the frig and a kettle as if she has only recently made acquaintance with them. I look out of the window and find myself checking out the moorland, the stone walls, and the sheep. And isn't that a kestrel hanging over the drive? Eventually, after brief embraces and handshakes, we get into the car. I recognise that Alice is slightly tearful. Perhaps I am too.

'Well. A successful little escapade,' Alice says flippantly as we drive away. 'We can now lip-read and sign if no one rushes us.'

'But you made huge progress, Alice. I'm hopeless.'

'But who made the biggest hit of the night with your Tuareg story,' she teases. 'All those fanciful reflections on geology and creativity. The ultimate philosophical puzzle and adventure. And you dazzled them in there with it.'

'Come on. George was a huge help. Anyhow, back to the sketchbooks. I've got a feeling that I know where I'm going with them.'

'Continuing the conversation eh! That Cass is a clever girl.'

'Absolutely. A conversation with all my landscapes. How's that for a title? "Conversations with the Earth." Or "the Rocks beneath our feet".' Then after a pause, 'You know throughout our whole stay here I haven't had one dizzy spell. Even the tinnitus is manageable. And yet my head sometimes spins with all the words and signs we've picked up. Amazing that a couple like George and Cass can teach us old ones a lesson. In more than signing.'

'Four lessons really. First the signing. Then how to be observant of things, just ordinary things. Then Cass with her idea for you of a "conversation with the Tuareg". A lastly how to enjoy a good meal and make love again.'

'Careful. That certainly wasn't in the brochure. We don't know anything about *their* love life.'

'I'm willing to bank on it being as good as ours.'

***

We have a week or so at home before Joanne announces a visit. She will be bringing Petr. Alice and I have fun signing with each other though it is all done rather frivolously. I'm still amazed at how seriously Alice takes it… and yet I'm likely to be the main beneficiary.

Joanne has told us how serious Petr is and golly she's right. He's wearing a grey suit and a grey tie, black shoes. He watches me as I speak, as if weighing up my words, and then speaks to me directly and slowly, the way the official pamphlets advise people to address the deaf, and I certainly get the gist of what he is saying, better than I do with Joanne.

I still have the sound of her voice inside my head, and it is a lovely one… I suppose that's her father speaking… but I miss the actual words. In the end, she uses the pad like Alice, and we make some progress. Alice and I do a quick demonstration of signing, though I suspect the clarity of our signing would not have passed the test with Cass.

We go out for our usual walks, enjoy a meal at a pub, and visit local museums and churches. Petr is a great observer, his inspection of everything in a museum or even in gardens is never cursory. In the evening, he and Joanne play arrangements of Bach's Two & Three Part Inventions. "Arrangement" is not the right technical word. One plays the right hand, the other plays the left. It makes for a very intimate music-making.

Once, just for fun, Joanne sat to the left but played the right-hand part, and he played the bass from the right-hand side, their wrists lying across each other. And that makes even Petr laugh at last, especially when signals get mixed and things break down. Otherwise, he is almost too polite and chivalrous towards Joanne. What on earth would he make of Thomas and the dynamic Tig?

On their last evening, suddenly, Petr asks in a very formal way, if he may marry Joanne. But it will not be straight away. He explains it all to Alice. He will finish his course and then he will be applying for various teaching posts in the Czech Republic.

Joanne has agreed to join him there and find work as a doctor. Are Alice and I willing to allow that? Alice comes back to me with a précis of all this. I say that the decision is up to Joanne. Will it be easy for her to find work as a doctor there? What about language?

It transpires that Joanne is learning Czech anyway. They seem to be quite decided that it is what they want. Joanne explains that it is a decision that both have made, of course. Petr wants to pursue his composition in his homeland… he says that the culture, even the forests and rocks and soil of the country… are embedded in it. (As a geologist, how could I not admire that sentiment?) Meanwhile, Joanne is certain that she wants to be an ordinary family doctor at the moment.

It doesn't really matter where she does that. People's ailments are pretty non-specific as to location. In Europe at least. So it's logical that they should for the time being choose the Czech Republic. They may have different ideas in the future.

Of course, we give them our blessing, Alice with formal words to match Petr's and me with handshakes and hugs. Again, I suspect that I am close to tears. Having partly lost my daughter to deafness, I am likely to lose even more of her to geography. Invitations to visit Petr's family in the Republic follow. Who am I to complain about the distance? The Czech Republic is a short flight away or just a longish rail journey.

Once they have gone back to London, Alice and I have the house to ourselves and quite a lot to think about. But the edgy anxiety that has plagued me for the past months seems to have evaporated. Even Alice says she is in a positive frame of mind about working with the three universities.

'I think the four of them are going to be alright,' she says. 'Our two offspring and their partners. And we will manage, won't we? That farm did something for us didn't it?' And she flicked the word "acceptance" in my direction (an open hand stretched out in front which encloses, like someone holding something fragile, a bird's egg, a tiny frog, a loose diamond). I give her my usual thumbs-up. It is the only sign that I could employ with complete immediacy and confidence.

18

Harry
Twelve Months Later

We have a cottage close to Lochinver in North-West Scotland. Two weeks of quietness we can share. This place is a geologist's heaven. But more than that, it's the right place for both of us. I am working on what might be the last chapter of my book on Landscapes; Alice is working on her book on the Brain and Music.

We manage one meal out at a loch-side hotel, but otherwise, we self-cater with a big emphasis on frozen ready-meals. There are long walks in the morning unless it is raining, and we spend the afternoons and rainy days on our projects. Mine sometimes takes me out again in the afternoons while Alice works on her book in the cottage or in the garden.

The geology project has at last taken centre stage for me. I have collated most of my photographs diagrams and notes and have started to write a series of monographs. I have already visited Shropshire, the Norfolk Coast and Snowdonia. Wherever I stay, usually at a pub, I make it quite clear at the outset that I am completely deaf. It's not strictly true… I can pick up louder sounds, but speech is a closed book for me.

Of course, I lip-read and read gestures. After a fashion, once in a while, I meet someone who can sign. It's not often that they can understand my signed gibberish. Alice encourages me in the kind of obstinacy that conducts these trips on my own. The vertigo has gone, for good I hope.

Even the tinnitus is an unintrusive companion. Thomas took time off to accompany me to Norfolk, and we had a fine time scrambling through mud channels and striding along shingle beaches. When I was staying at Bettws Coed, Joanne and Petr dropped in on me, and I was able to give the very receptive Petr a guided tour and lecture on glaciation features. He says it will prove invaluable when he next visits the mountains on the Czech-German border. I have been to the Yorkshire Dales again, on my own, and there were no low-flying aircraft (unless I just didn't hear them).

And, finally, there was Shropshire, a discontinuous maze of rocks forming the Church Stretton fault, the Long Mynde, and the strange quartzite "tors", the Stipperstones.

Now, we are here in Scotland and Alice is with me, which makes it a real holiday. We do a lot of walking, in between showers. There are also great swathes of time when we can ignore the geology, and enjoy the heather, the sea birds, and eagles, the islands on the horizon, and the smell of sea-water bracken and peat. There are small harbour towns and stone-age forts to visit, and welcoming pubs.

A week ago, Alice and I were sitting in a cafe in Kyle of Lochalsh. Three guys and a girl in their twenties occupied a nearby table. They were in a highly animated mood regaling each other with stories and jokes. The menu on a huge card attracted their special attention. They pointed at items and then obviously added their own comments, not many of them complimentary. Alice and I watched open-mouthed because it was all signed.

We finished our meal, paid for it, and walked away in silence.

'So what was all that about?' Alice mouthed to me.

I shook my head. It was all too fast and furious.

'Was it even in English?' I asked. Alice seemed to think it was, though perhaps with a Scottish accent. Somehow what they had to say was expressed in the whole operatic performance of gestures and facial expressions. Rarely had I seen a menu evaluated, or was it damned, so thoroughly.

'Will we ever get to that level,' I say to Alice.

'Only if we go back to being children.'

'But they were adults. In their twenties.'

'Still children at heart,' she signs to me with two quick gestures which I understand immediately.

My aim now is to complete an illustrated book suitable for the traveller about underlying geology and the geomorphic process visible in the landscape. Britain after all is geologically a land of extremes. Everywhere there are ancient platforms of rock created by magma, then alluvial plains, evidence of tropical seas, deserts, and glaciated uplands. Just think of those injections of magma and outpourings of lava which can be seen in the Islands of the Arran and Mull further south.

Then in front of our eyes is the massive platform of ancient igneous Lewisian gneiss on which we are perched at this moment, while scattered about us are these isolated and gnome-like mountain tops of quartz and Torridonian sandstone. Real desert material. The remnants are gritty sandstones with dramatic peaks like Suilven, Stac Polly and my favourite, Liathach, the old grey one.

It shares that otherworldly character of those piles of rock and scarps in Niger. But this landscape has been scraped, scrubbed and scoured by glaciers and ice sheets to produce a different but equally uncompromisingly beautiful landscape, Title of book undecided, Conversations with? Or is that too corny?

I have begun also to read some of the poetry that Joanne and Alice have prescribed for me. One day I may work out how it might be included in another book, or at least lines may be used as chapter headings. I have drawn a line against introducing music references. It would be dishonest to wax eloquent on something I cannot hear nor remember. I leave all that side to Alice.

I have wondered about travelling abroad, Yugoslavia, Iceland, Sicily. Actually, I fancy a series of geological portraits of islands. Most of the European ones manage to pack a lot of dramatic geology into a comparatively small space. Think of Sicily, Corsica, Crete.

Of course, above all, I ought to write a definitive monograph on the wadi in Niger. I owe it to that group of Tuareg who were entombed there. Perhaps I will one day. But I'm not sure whether it would be a scientific study. There will certainly not be a re-visit.

Declan sent me a copy of his full report on Niger. All figures, diagrams and scientific observations. No whiff of the trials and tribulations of nomadic life with only a passing reference to the rockfall. The noble isolation of the Tuareg and the splendour of the evening landscapes, are all passed

141

by. My pre-rockfall sketch of the Escarpment is on the cover of Declan's report. With my permission of course.

So the triple confrontation I have had with the uncertainties of my and indeed all life: the Niger tragedy, my son's disgrace and my own deafness, are now behind me. Not resolved in the conventional sense. The Tuareg are still buried and uncelebrated; Thomas is hopefully on a healthier career path but a risky one with Tig on his heels; my deafness is more or less complete and my lip-reading and signing juvenile. Joanne is married and not really so far away in the Czech Republic. I hesitate to use words like nemesis, or destiny… I think they are escapes from the reality. But I think I am now taking life's uncertainties in my stride.

Alice meanwhile is working on her book. She has a wider audience in mind not just an academic one. It hovers over the boundary between music psychology and medicine, but she would like parents, care workers and the general public to read it. But its aim is to show how our brains hear music, our ears being merely a portal. How and why we respond to music in the way we do.

Whenever our ears pick up and transmit sounds to the brain, a huge number of departments seem to be involved. One of them is the hippocampus, where the memory of all the music we have already heard throughout our lives is stored away. And the way we respond to music is influenced by that huge legacy. Two people sitting listening to the same piece of music will hear different sounds.

We aren't blank sheets. Professionals and therapists will have to work out how this understanding can be applied especially to children and adults with autism or with other mental disabilities. The aim is to bring more musical light into those individuals' troubled darkness. Tapping into each person's hidden music library. It seems to me that there is a parallel between geology (and geomorphology) and music. They underlie and support.

They move forward... the music flows, and the landscape is slowly modelled and changed. Both may have their outbursts, fortissimo and dissonance. The record may come to an end but neither the music nor the geology stops, Cadences are only temporary affairs. There's always something new on the horizon, which is tenuously connected with the present.

It makes me think about the role of the conductor of a symphony orchestra, or even of Petr with his contemplative arrhythmic music, (or so it seems to me) or George with his lexicon of signs for birds. Connections, always connections. Leading to other connections. None of them were completed or in isolation. Works in progress.

I once accused Alice of making a fetish of incompleteness, or the word "unresolvability" (which I have probably coined), She was almost angry with me. 'If you've nothing else to do, try counting up the number of times that the word "perhaps" comes into most scientific findings. Not one of the people who come into our lab goes away magically "restored" in the physical sense, but they might as a result of what we do, gain some comfort. Our findings may help them to find comfort.

'Yet nothing we do or write is fixed or prescriptive. Just pointers. Sometimes guesses. In ten years or even earlier someone will be exposing the inaccuracy or incompleteness of what has been written. That's as it should be.'

However, while we are here in Scotland, she says her work is going well. Those obstinately knobbly hills on the horizon, the gentle swash of the waves on the sea-shore are a great stimulus. And we are comfortable with each other again. Now that I don't lean on Alice for some kind of validation of my mental turmoil, things are better between us. And I can take a real interest in her work. Is it really so different from what I am attempting with this book of mine?

Incidentally, I wonder if I could dedicate my book to that Tuareg lad. First books usually get dedicated to a supportive wife; I have had that in abundance. But somehow the Tuareg lad deserves the accolade and Alice will understand.

Joanne e-mails and writes to us from the Czech Republic. They were married there six months ago, and we attended the wedding. Very formal and beautiful. While we were there, she gave me a wedding present too. Why not, she said.

The bride's parents deserve a bit of fuss too. It is a CD of a piece called Desert by Varese. For Alice, there is a book of poetry by Edwin Muir. 'I've put a book marker in for the poem, *The Horses*. You both should read it.'

Joanne has a hospital job and enjoys it though she says she would like one day to return to general practice. Her Czech is coming on well, but Petr is inundated with teaching and administrative work and complains that his composing time is threatened. But things will change eventually, some of the admin will move over to a colleague, and he will be able to get his head down, his hands back on the keyboard.

'And by the way,' she says. 'Before I forget, I am expecting a baby in six months' time.'

I don't know which of us is more delighted with that last piece of news.

Thomas is still difficult to pin down. Central Africa is his present location while Tig is organising protests here in

Britain. I don't think marriage and babies are on their agendas. It is unclear what Tig's attitude to such conventional domestic matters affairs might be.

But, when I compare Thomas's situation now with the one in London over a year ago, I am grateful. A few months back, he appeared on a TV programme about the environment... as some sort of pundit. Or at least as someone who has got his hands dirty at the environmental rock-face as we geologists would say. The usual messy metaphors.

What will emerge in the next stage of the lives of the four of us? Well, seven actually, if I include spouses and the unborn child. I am not always on the lookout for resolution and finality any more.

We wonder how Cass and George are getting on with their lives. Are they inspiring other deaf people with the words, the signs, the birds and the bees?

As the clown sang in *Twelfth Night*, 'What's to come is still unsure.'